Praise for *The Day the Rains Came*

"David Wolinsky's *The Day the Rains Came*, his new well-crafted and imaginative collection of short stories, is funny, irreverent, sometimes surprising, and, above all, highly entertaining. I count it as offering some of the best Jewish humor of recent times. Step aside, Mel Brooks!"

— Philip Slayton, bestselling author and Rhodes Scholar

"I have known badass humor-writer David Wolinsky for just under a decade. Once, his erudite wit caused me to publicly snort chicken noodle soup out of my nose…but I was innocent, his insane brand of funny was the culprit."

— Frannie Sheridan, actress, humorist, and author of
Confessions of a Jewish Shiksa

"What do Klaatu the alien, Sebastian the assassin, the late Orville Redenbacher, and the planet Xngpilzian have in common? The answer: they all appear in this book, which springs from the fertile if somewhat twisted, imagination of one David Wolinsky, a retired lawyer, restauranteur, and Canadian army officer. What Mr. Wolinsky has clearly not retired from is humor, which is the ingredient shared by this bizarre but delightful collection of short stories. This is no ordinary book of short stories. It's funnier!!!"

— Michael Posner, award-winning writer, playwright,
journalist, and author of three volumes of
Leonard Cohen, Untold Stories

"David Wolinsky was, allegedly, an entertainment lawyer in a previous life, which may explain why the stories in this volume often involve TV shows, scripts and 'treatments,' movies, music, the Fox network, and Los Angeles. Or maybe it's the other way around. Everyone in Hollywood supposedly has a headshot or a screenplay. Wolinsky is not known to have a headshot, but his literary aspirations are familiar to all the recipients of his morning memos and random musings. They come to fruition in this volume.

His cast of characters is Chaucerian. In this engaging collection of vignettes and short stories, you will find actors, rappers, gamblers, detectives, Mafia hitmen, supernatural visitors, interstellar visitors, talking birds, a long-suffering baker, Donald and Hillary, Orville Redenbacher, and Frank Sinatra. English majors will also note a certain stylistic range: shaggy dog stories, Jewish jokes, rants and grievances, and feghoots — stories that end in a pun.

David's preoccupation with both puns and baked goods stems from a childhood experience of entering a raffle for what he thought was a Winnebago. His joy upon drawing the lucky number turned to chagrin when he went to claim the prize and discovered that instead of a camper van, it was a raffle to Win a Bagel. Musing on this rye mistake, he resolved henceforth to never Win a Peg, watch out for sparking pots, and always listen for wordplay. His bio lists him as a former member of Mensa. It is not known whether punning is a symptom or a cause of his loss of eligibility for membership, but it hasn't hurt his writing at all."

— Gregory Guy, Professor of Linguistics, New York University

The author is a retired army officer, entertainment attorney, restauranteur, businessman and currently a writer. He is a former member of Mensa and the Alliance of Cinema, Television and Radio Artists. He has three sons, the eldest an accomplished Assistant U.S. Attorney for California, his middle son an international award-winning Creative Director for a major iconic company, and his youngest, a successful corporate attorney, businessman, and professional, consummate executive chef.

The author lives in the Pacific Northwest with his cat Barney.

The Day
The Rains Came

The Day
The Rains Came

By
David Wolinsky

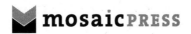

Library and Archives Canada Cataloguing in Publication

Title: The day the rains came / by David Wolinsky.

Names: Wolinsky, David (Retired lawyer), author.

Description: Short stories.

Identifiers: Canadiana (print) 20240284178
Canadiana (ebook) 20240284186

ISBN 9781771617246 (softcover) ISBN 9781771617253 (PDF)
ISBN 9781771617260 (EPUB) ISBN 9781771617277 (Kindle)

Subjects: LCGFT: Flash fiction.
Classification: LCC PS8645.O452 D39 2024 | DDC C813/.6—dc23

Published by Mosaic Press, Oakville, Ontario, Canada, 2024.
MOSAIC PRESS, Publishers
www.Mosaic-Press.com
Copyright © David Wolinsky 2024

Printed and bound in Canada.

MOSAIC PRESS
1252 Speers Road, Units 1 & 2, Oakville, Ontario, L6L 5N9 (905) 825-2130
info@mosaic-press.com • www.mosaic-press.com

For Linda

Contents

Prologue

Many years ago, while trolling through the internet, I came across a series of personal ads ostensibly culled from the classified sections of Israel's newspapers. These included:

"I am a sensitive Jewish prince whom you can open your heart to. Share your innermost thoughts and deepest secrets. Confide in me. I'll understand your insecurities. No fatties, please."

"Jewish male, 34, very successful, smart, independent, self-made. Looking for a girl whose father will hire me."

"Single Jewish woman, 29, into disco, mountain climbing, skiing, track, and field. Has slight limp."

"Divorced Jewish man, seeks partner to attend Schule with, light Shabbos candles, celebrate holidays, build sukkah together, attend Brisses, Bar Mitzvahs. Religion not important."

"Israeli professor, 41, with 18 years of teaching in my behind. Looking for American-born woman who speaks English very good."

Humor is to Jews what a dram of whiskey and a song is to the Irish, precision is to the Germans and an affair is to the French. Across the millennia, those who have attempted to eradicate the Jews would have been more successful if they had banned humor rather than synagogues or prayer. Just twenty-two years after the Holocaust, the brilliant Mel Brooks came out with the film *The Producers* which ultimately became one of the highest grossing Broadway musical comedies ever. It of course featured the song *Springtime for Hitler*. I know of no other religion that could have found humor in such an horrendous event so soon after its occurrence.

Whether it's because of millennia of persecution or just something genetic, Jews will as a last resort always turn to humor and will rarely allow themselves to be offended by even the most outlandish.

My principal fear in writing this book was that my friends and family would think I had gone Hollywood, was no longer the warm, caring, lovely person I had always been, and now considered myself the second coming of Tolstoy. Which, of course, was foolishness.

And yet, there are certain inescapable comparisons. Tolstoy was the spiritual son of Russian Aristocracy, and I am a sensitive Jewish Prince. Tolstoy served as a Second Lieutenant artillery officer as did I, and was then promoted to First Lieutenant, as was I. We both studied Law. We both can be classified as distinguished elder statesmen with beards. We both had stories the world waited anxiously to hear. And finally, Tolstoy had an ineffable, warm, loving sense of humor, much like my own. On the eve of his marriage, he gave his bride to be his diaries detailing his extensive sexual past, and the fact that one of the serfs on his estate had borne him a son. Such a kidder, and certainly had I been alive then, something over which we could have bonded. I had considered calling this book 'War in Pieces" after I was awakened in the middle of the night by what I can only conclude was Tolstoy's ghost, screaming at me that it was time for me to reconsider the title.

Most people spend their life pursuing one vocation. I have battled through six different callings, army officer, attorney, entertainment consultant, restauranteur, businessman, and finally writer. And so after Tolstoy's imprecation, it occurred to me that indeed, my life had been a history of war in pieces, and the stories in this book are the detritus still wallowing in my head at the conclusion of these struggles. Ultimately, however I decided to retain the original title, for no other reason than fear of Tolstoy's descendants claiming part of my meager royalties.

In my younger days, there was a city councillor who was famous for his malapropisms, such as *"You buttered your bread, now lie in it."* I mentioned all the foregoing, so that you might be forewarned that certain of the following stories may not be politically correct or even in good taste, but when it comes to humor, for Jews, nothing is sacred. Hopefully you will at least find them to be amusing. In any event, you've been cautioned. If you choose to proceed, well then, you've buttered your bread, now lie in it.

Chapter One

I Am a Sensitive Jewish Prince

My son nearly broke my heart. There, I've said it. I love all my sons. They are each brilliant, moral, kind, generous, funny, considerate, and generally, incredible young men. They worked hard from an early age, self-motivated, asked and expected nothing and each achieved incredible success in their chosen fields of endeavor. Plus they tolerated the insanities of their father with gentle acceptance. But truth is truth, and one of my sons very nearly killed me. To better understand, you'll require a little history.

As far back as I can remember, (and being near eidetic, that would be to the delivery room when the doctor turned to a nurse and remarked 'Fat little bugger, isn't he?') I have been a loner. Never part of any group, gang, club, team, clique, association, or other gathering of people normally part of the social fabric. It wasn't a question of acceptance, more of preference. I have always enjoyed being by myself, an outsider so to speak. Off to the side, observing the world as it passed before him. When you would go to a social event of any type, a wedding, Bar Mitzvah, anniversary, Christmas, or New Year's party, I would be the one standing off to the side with a cup of coffee in my hand, a smile on my face, observing the event transpiring around him.

At a very early age I became aware of this predilection and for a while it concerned me. Then I noticed that I resembled neither of my parents nor my older sister nor in fact any other member of my extended family. It was at that point that I came to the only logical conclusion. On the day I was born, there must have been some woman of royal lineage passing through our city who chose at that moment in time to go into labor. Somehow, in what may have been the origin of the term "royal screw-up", two babies were mixed up, and some hick from the prairies went back to Europe with my parents and I was left to fend for myself with his natural parents. And please don't misunderstand me. I loved my adoptive parents. My adoptive parents were Jewish. My adoptive father was the original gentleman attorney, beloved by his huge clientele, with never an ill word for anyone. My adoptive mother was a brilliant and incredibly funny feminist, ahead of her time, heading numerous charitable and political organizations. But both were still, how can I put this kindly, commoners. Somewhere in Europe I knew there was a royal family constantly wondering why their son occasionally lapsed into Yiddish.

I have always been pragmatic and so I accepted the situation and chose to make the best of it that I could. I did my best to be a good son, attentive to my adoptive parents needs, worked hard and, where necessary, mingled with others, but always reluctantly, since generally I was happier on my own. Although I could have opted for a life of hermitage to indulge my preference, I did not. Soldier, attorney, restaurateur, businessman all required a modicum of social relationships, and I never eschewed the required interaction. But still, my royal blood precluded me from ever joining in whole heartedly. I was born to a higher level, to observe, assist when required, but otherwise remain aloof.

And then my son nearly broke my heart. I don't think for a minute it was intentional, but what is, is. My middle son is an advertising genius. He was declared to be the number one under thirty advertising man in the world by Business Insider. The same year, he won the *Platinum Lion* at Cannes for the best advertising campaign in the world. Shortly thereafter, he was considering taking on a new client, one of the genetic testing websites and suggested that he and I should subscribe for a DNA test. I resisted at first, afraid that once he found out that what he thought was his heritage was in fact a lie, he might lose all faith. Nonetheless I acceded to his request. And the results were conclusive. Our DNA was 97% Ashkenazi, European Jews. Moreover, the site referred us to several relatives, children of my adoptive father's siblings who also shared our DNA. Which meant of course that my adoptive mother and father were in fact my real parents and my lifelong illusions were no more than that, illusions.

For days I never left my condo. I refused to answer the phone or texts or emails. My heart was nearly broken. My entire life had been a sham. And then suddenly, realization struck me. Somewhere in my heritage, perhaps even dating back to the twelve tribes of Israel, there was nobility. It may have skipped hundreds or even thousands of generations, but ultimately the royal genes had made their way to my sensitive soul. Royalty may have skipped generations, but there was no mistaking it for what it was. I am a sensitive Jewish Prince and accept it proudly. I shall pursue this heritage now on Anscestry.com, and no matter how long it takes, I shall ultimately determine who in my lineage ruled what country and when.

One final note. As and when I do determine the origin of my royal blood, I shall be the same humble, sensitive person I presently am. I shall require neither genuflecting nor hereditary titles. You may still address me as David. although I wouldn't look on it unkindly if you chose to include a respectful "Sir" after pronouncing my given name.

Chapter Two

The Day the Earth Stood Stiller

Vestron 23578

It was an ingenious idea, but not surprising since the members of the council were at a minimum two million years more evolved than the Neanderthals presently under discussion.

The planet called Earth in the Milky Way Galaxy had first come to the attention of the responsible members of the World Allied Leaders Managing Aboriginal Regional Territories (WALMART) when a normal scan of that section of the universe indicated growing unrest and the possibility of potential global conflict on that planet. It had been a week ago Tuesday on Vestron, or 1939 on Earth in the space-time continuum. Although general policy dictated against interference, there was a feeling that at least a minimal warning should be provided as a courtesy. All were agreed that such a primitive, somewhat aggressive, and seemingly irrational assembly of humanity didn't merit the expenditure of an actual visit, but still, there was agreement that something should be done. It was Klaatu who had come up with the solution and had, with the concurrence of the rest of the Council members, immediately put it into effect.

The plan was simple. Utilizing an earthling selected at random, an American writer named Harry Bates, Klaatu imbedded in Bates's mind a story which was subsequently published in the October issue of *Astounding Science Fiction* under the title *Farewell to the Master*. The story was told from the viewpoint of a free-lance reporter who witnesses the arrival of an alien spaceship on the grounds of the U.S. Capital. A god-like person emerges from the ship together with an eight-foot-tall robot. The person only manages to say "I am Klaatu and this is Gnot" before he is shot and killed by a lunatic. What follows are efforts by Gnot to recover part of Klaatu and replicate his life form, while Sutherland, a reporter embarks on a series of adventures, interacts with Gnot and tries to explain that Gnot's master's death was an accident, until Gnot replies, "You misunderstand. I am the master." The whole intended purpose of the story was to convey to the barbarians on the planet Earth the reality of their situation. They were meaningless. There were civilizations in the universe light years ahead of them intellectually, who had in fact ceded control of enforcement of universal safety to an agency of all powerful robots, thereby removing the danger of irrational behavior from the equation.

Sadly, the message failed to get across and a world war ensued on the planet. The following day, or 1949, in the

Earth's time-space continuum, Klaatu realized that his initial effort had failed, that Earth was on the brink of another major confrontation in Korea, and he implanted a subsequent story in the mind of Edmund H. North who created a screenplay which was subsequently released in 1951 as a movie, *The Day the Earth Stood Still*. This time around, the spaceship lands again in Washington, and Klaatu emerges to announce that he is visiting the earth in peace. When he attempts to reveal a gift that would have enabled the people of Earth to study life on other planets, he is shot by one of the soldiers surrounding the spaceship. An eight-foot-tall robot now named Gort emerges from the spaceship and disintegrates the offending soldier, but Klaatu then orders him to desist. Klaatu is taken to the hospital where after surgery, he uses some miracle salve to heal himself and then manages to sneak away and embarks on a series of adventures before returning to his spaceship where, when he next emerges, he is once again shot and killed. Gort manages to retrieve his body, bring him back inside the ship where he is brought back to life, temporarily. Klaatu then emerges and explains to the people of earth that their time is limited unless they change their ways. He explains about how the governing body of robots will enforce order in the universe and destroy the planet Earth unless there are changes. He then departs.

The following Tuesday, or 2007 in Earth time, it became apparent to the Council that all previous efforts had failed. Earth was engaged in major battles in Iraq, Afghanistan, Africa, the Middle East, unrest in certain parts of South America and there was the emergence of a powerful group of media crazies utilizing a wolf like creature as their network title. Moreover, the planet now had a proliferation of nuclear weapons. The consensus of the Council was that the situation was hopeless, but Klaatu argued and prevailed and was given one final chance to implement a change through his mind melding technique. Accordingly, he implanted a concept in the mind of David Scarpa who created a screenplay for a film which was released in 2008 under the same title, *The Day the Earth Stood Still*.

This time around, the spaceship lands in Central Park. (Klaatu felt that New Yorkers might be a more enlightened and receptive audience for his message.) Once again, Klaatu is shot by some aggressive member of the U.S. military, Gort emerges to rescue him and exact revenge but is temporarily restrained by Klaatu. There ensues a series of incidents involving Klaatu and sympathetic as well as crazy or disturbed earthlings, all the while Klaatu is trying to get across the message that he must finish his mission to save the Earth. Despite these efforts, all hell breaks loose, Klaatu manages to call off Gort and save the world from his wrath, only to be killed once again himself. After saving humanity, Klaatu is consumed by the conflagration he managed to stop, having time only to warn that "there will be a price to the human way of life" which turns out to be the cessation all electrical activity on Earth. The spaceship then departs.

The next morning, or 2018, Earth time, it was obvious to all that Klaatu's last, desperate effort had failed. Not only had the conflicts on Earth continued, but there was also now talk of weaponizing space. Because of the empathy he had developed for this miserable planet, despite all its resistance to his efforts, Klaatu pleaded with Council to permit him one last chance. Rather than implanting any suggestions in the minds of any of the Earth idiots, he himself would travel in person to the planet and deliver the final ultimatum. This was met with a great deal of resistance. Firstly, it was a breach of the prime directive. More important, based on the historical evidence, it would most likely prove unproductive. Klaatu argued however that it would take less time for him to travel to Earth to deliver the message than it might to write the report for the rest of WALMART detailing their failure. By a vote of 15 to 14, Klaatu was dispatched to Earth.

Klaatu's spaceship landed in Central Park as per the last episode. Once again, he emerged from the ship to announce that he had come in peace, only this time he was there in person. He managed to get out "I am here on a mission of peace to save the" before he was shot by a nervous soldier. Gort attempted to intercede but was restrained by Klaatu. Klaatu was rushed to Mount Sinai Hospital where he was operated on and again, applied his wonder salve. (One of the hospital doctors maintained the salve was just *Polysporin*, but his knowledge was based on hearsay provided to him by one of the attending nurses who had imparted this information to him while he was boffing her in one of the hospital's linen closets.)

While Klaatu was recovering, despite the recommendation of his National Security Adviser that he should just nuke the hospital, the President visited Klaatu and brought him a "*Make America Great Again*" hat as a gift. Then to break the ice asked,

"Do you come here often?" and finally offered to sell him a condo in Trump Tower at an extremely beneficial price (cash only) so that he could have a place to stay while in town and on future visits. They began to discuss why Klaatu had come, but unfortunately the hospital only carried Diet Pepsi, not Diet Coke so the President had to leave before these discussions could be concluded but promised he would return.

After recovering thanks to his wonder salve, Klaatu managed to escape from the hospital while his guards' attention was diverted by two of the nurses discussing what they had observed about his physiology while Klaatu was undergoing surgery, to the effect that they doubted that the eight-foot Gort was more blessed than Klaatu in the "Joe Cocker" department. After leaving the hospital, utilizing minimal disguises to protect himself from discovery, Klaatu embarked on a mission to try and discover just what it was that made these crazy Earthlings tick and whether in fact it was worth all the effort to try and save them.

For the next three days, while much of the world was searching for him, Klaatu moved unnoticed around Manhattan, trying to intuit a better understanding of the planet's inhabitants. From the street vendors, taxi drivers, restaurant and store personnel and the myriad of the general population, of different races, religions, and heritage, all rushing to be somewhere else, he observed that they often seemed impatient, angry, distressed, belligerent and unhappy. And yet, confronted individually, they were generally kind, considerate, tolerant, thoughtful and, in many cases, quite funny.

He visited a church, a mosque, a synagogue, a half dozen ethnic restaurants and two museums. Later, back in his hotel room, he watched a local cable channel that was running 24 hours of Stiller and Stiller, TV shows of Jerry Stiller, such as *The Paul Lynde Show, Rhoda and Seinfeld* interspersed with films and television shows of Ben Stiller such as *Arrested Development, Saturday Night Live, Curb your Enthusiasm, Zoolander and Little Folkers*.

Much to his own amazement, he discovered a side of these people he had not realized existed. Despite their primitive nature, their inability to control their emotions or restrict their unhealthy proclivities, there was something inherently endearing about them and worthy of permitting them perhaps another 50 or so years to see if perhaps they could surmount their demons and avoid self immolation. Concluding that there was little purpose in remaining on the planet any longer, he decided to return to his ship before these bastards killed him once again and so he did. With Gort's protection, he managed to board the ship and return home before they even realized he was gone. Which in a way was a pity, as the President was prepared to offer him an opportunity to have the 18th hole at Turnberry in Scotland renamed Klaatu's Klincher in exchange for an endorsement in the upcoming election.

I should point out that I have no idea where the idea for this chapter came from. I had started to type a chapter about the migrating habits of Canadian geese and when I finished and went back to read it, *The Day the Earth Stood Stiller* was what I had written. I suppose that it's possible Klaatu decided on one more mind meld rather than a personal visitation for which, who could really blame him. A man can only be killed so many times before he gets royally pissed. Hopefully, we have another fifty years to work things out.

Chapter Three

Proposition Paulie

Paulie was a good soul. Truly. He wasn't one of life's great achievers, but then how many of life's great achievers are good souls.

Paulie believed in God. His father was a simple factory worker Protestant, and his mother was a stay at home staunch Catholic. In case you don't know the difference between a Catholic and a staunch Catholic, a staunch Catholic lying in bed at night instinctively makes a cross asking forgiveness after farting even though still fast asleep.

Paulie's mother and father agreed prior to Paulie's birth that he would be allowed to choose his own religious denomination without any persuasion from either parent. This didn't stop either of them however from debating the merits of both schools of thought during breakfast, lunch, and dinner almost every day. Although meals might start with questions about what the day held for one another, conversations quickly deteriorated into vociferous contention as to the credibility of J.J. (Just Jesus) as opposed to MSHG (Mother, Son and Holy Ghost). In later years, Paulie always insisted any restaurant food he ordered be free of M.S.G. as he felt this possibly referred to Mother, Son and Ghost. Ultimately, Paulie opted for the Church of Paulie and God, without any middleman, woman, or ghost.

Paulie always listened to and respected his teachers. Their words were gospel. In the fourth grade, Paulie's English teacher was a lovely lady by the name of Selma Whibble. Although he was extremely fond of Mrs. Whibble, he was not a huge fan of English class, since English was only his second language, Brooklynese being his first. Mrs. Whibble had been talking to the class about the myth of what was commonly referred to as the stranded preposition. In English grammar, preposition stranding refers to a syntactic construction in which a preposition is left without a following object. A stranded preposition most often appears at the end of a sentence, although it's not unusual to find one at the beginning of a sentence as well.

An example of a stranded preposition at the end of a sentence would be "Who were you talking to?" Strict grammarians would suggest that proper English would be "To whom were you talking?"

An example of a stranded preposition at the beginning of a sentence would be "Outside, being close to midnight, all good teenagers should have been in the house in bed." Good grammarians would suggest that proper English would be

"All good teenagers should have been in bed, since outside the house it was close to midnight." Of course they would all be better served by worrying about whether their teenagers were in bed by themselves at midnight rather than the stranded preposition but that's neither here nor there.

Mrs. Whibble was telling her class that the stranded preposition was in fact a myth in the modern English language and that it was often totally acceptable, if not preferable to either start or end a sentence with a preposition. The problem was that Paulie's mother and father had been debating the Eucharist at breakfast that morning and all the attendant talk about eating the body and drinking the blood of Christ had seriously grossed out Paulie who had difficulty eating any form of meat that was less than charbroiled. So while Mrs. Whibble was rambling on about the stranded preposition, he had tuned her out and was trying to get the image of his mother nibbling on Jesus's ankle out of his mind. His attention only came back to the present when Mrs. Wibble declared that it was totally acceptable, if not preferable to either start or end a sentence with a proposition.

Paulie took it to heart and vowed to do his best to adhere to these words of wisdom. Now I should have mentioned that in addition to not being one of life's great intellectuals, Paulie also suffered from attention deficit syndrome and a mild hearing loss so while it's quite possible that Mrs. Whibble may in fact have said that it was often preferable to start and end a sentence with a 'proposition' rather than a 'preposition', it's also equally possible that it was just God with his inimitable sense of humor screwing with Paulie.

15

Any serious gambler will tell you that a proposition bet is almost always a sucker bet. Rather than betting on a single event, you are betting on a series of two or more events happening sequentially and if any one of such events fails to happen, you lose everything. What makes it a sucker bet is that even though with each added event your odds go up substantially, as a rule the reward never increases at a similar rate. If you choose rather than betting on a single event with two to one odds and instead bet on a series of events all happening, increasing the odds of such events all happening from two to one to one hundred to one, the chances are also excellent that the proposed reward being offered will now be sixty or seventy to one rather than the hundred to one to render them equivalent to the increased risk. Ergo, a sucker bet.

In addition to not being overly gifted intellectually, Paulie was also, somewhat challenged in the physical realm. At only five feet zero inches and one hundred pounds when he entered grade eight, he was easy prey for the school bullies who quickly sought to take advantage of the situation. It didn't help that his school was in one of the rougher areas of Brooklyn. Then one afternoon after being intimidated and harassed by one of the tougher of the toughs, he was approached by one of the larger, meaner grade ten students who said "I've got a proposition. You give me one quarter of your lunch money every day and I'll make sure that nobody bothers you." Being pragmatic, as well as remembering what Mrs. Whibble had said about a sentence ending in a proposition being a good thing, Paulie quickly accepted the offer. Fortunately, he was able to take advantage of this arrangement right through grade 12 since his protector had to repeat two grades in the interim and was therefore part of Paulie's graduation class. If you could call it a graduation class for one month prior to the school graduation, his protector graduated to Riker's Island having been convicted of providing similar services to several of the neighborhood's smaller business establishments.

After completing grade 12, Paulie continued a life of mediocrity marked by neither satisfying employment nor relationship success, moving from one menial job to another and never stumbling on whomever fate had destined to be his mate. What marked Paulie throughout his life journey, however, was his adherence to Mrs. Whibble's cautionary advice. With the passage of time, he became renowned as an easy mark for any kind of proposition bet and whatever funds he was ever able to squirrel away, someone could always separate him from them with one proposition bet or another. His reputation grew as his assets diminished and he became known near and far as "Proposition Paulie".

When his parents passed and were finally able to determine who was right when they were met by either Jesus or the whole shebang, Mary, Jesus, and the guy in the sheet, they bequeathed Paulie their house, a small sum in the bank and the proceeds of a modest insurance policy. The predators were able to strip Paulie of the proceeds of the account and the insurance policy rather quickly with a number of ridiculous proposition bets, the pitch for which all should have been preceded by "Once upon a time" but try as they might, they were never able to convince him to sell, mortgage or bet the house since although he revered Mrs. Whibble, he had promised his parents before their demise that he would never in any way encumber or sell the house so that they could die knowing he would always have a place to live. Obviously just not knowing whether they were going to be met by JJ or MSHG was sufficient uncertainty for them to bear.

And thus, it remained until October 8th, 2016. It was the day after the release of Donald Trump's infamous 'Access Hollywood' tape. The Big Guy, came to visit while Paulie was sleeping and said "Paulie, you've been loyal and adhered to Mrs. Whibble's advice all these years, never once questioning it, so the time has come for you to reap the rewards. I want you to go to the bank and borrow the maximum amount you can against the house. Then I want you to fly to London and make the proposition bet of your lifetime. Bet the whole caboodle on Trump to win the presidential election, and the G.O.P. to win both the House and the Senate. But after you win, you can never make another proposition bet as long as you live." There is some possibility that in fact it wasn't God talking to Paulie, but rather the conversation he had heard the previous evening on television. He had just finished a sausage, pepperoni, red and green pepper, ham and pineapple pizza and had dozed off in front of the television while watching an interview on CNN during which one of the British contributors may have mentioned that after the *Access Hollywood* tape, the chances of Trump winning the White House or the GOP winning either the House or the Senate were less than zero and anyone looking to lose a fortune could never do better than making a proposition bet on Trump and the GOP winning all three.", but, any such suggestion that it wasn't God talking to Paulie would probably just be the bitter ramblings of an agnostic skeptic.

Never having any kind of credit problems, despite his proposition misfortunes, Paulie was able to convince his bank manager to advance him $300,000 against the house whose value had increased to at least $600,000. Paulie took a draft for the full sum and flew to London where he located the most reputable London Bookmaking establishment and approached them with his draft and his desire to bet on his election trifecta.

The owner of the business had to restrain himself from locking the shop's doors lest Paulie escape with his draft before signing the papers and the altruistic gentleman allowed himself to be cajoled into accepting the bet for the magnanimous odds of fifty to one. At the time, because of the *Access Hollywood* tape, as well as numerous allegations of Trump's sexual misconduct, the odds-on Trump winning the presidency had dropped to ten to one against. And because as Trump went, so did the House and Senate, the chances of the GOP winning either of these two were currently three to one against. Accordingly, on pure mathematics, a proposition bet on all three happening should have been ten times three times three, as if you had bet on one, taken the proceeds and bet on the second and then taken the proceeds and bet all of it on the third for a grand total of odds of ninety to one. But magnanimity does have its limits, so the establishment only allowed Paulie to cajole them into accepting his $300,000 draft based on odds of fifty to one, protesting all the time that 'WHEN' he won, they would have to come up with the enormous sum of more than fifteen million dollars. U.S., or as the owner of the book put it, "Son, if you're as sharp as I fear you are, you're going to clean us out."

Two months later Paulie's bank received a wire transfer of fifteen million U.S. and Paulie, true to his word, quit his job, invested the money in government bonds, and began travelling the world to see all the things he had previously missed. And he never again made a bet.

Until the spring of 2017. Once again, the Big Guy visited Paulie in his sleep and told him "Paulie, I've a great proposition for you. There's this public company called *Moviepass* which is offering a deal where you subscribe for $9.00 a month and can see as many movies during the month as you want. You love movies so you more than others can see what a fabulous deal this is. You are guaranteed that this company will take off like a rocket and despite what I told you previously, this is too good to pass up." Once again, the night before, Paulie had fallen asleep in front of the television just before an ad for *Moviepass* came on the screen, but it was likely that this was just a coincidence rather than the Big Guy not talking to Paulie. Regardless, Paulie was a believer so the next day he acted on the advice.

It was the following summer when *Moviepass* encountered difficulties in meeting their obligations with theatres and became unable to make their required payments, it appeared the deal was indeed too good to be true. people were going to more movies each month than had been anticipated and the value of the company's stock plummeted overnight, its shares losing $132 dollars per share of their value and reducing them at best to a penny stock worth not a great deal more than the paper on which they were printed.

Paulie was devastated. It wasn't that this would materially change his life since when he had awakened the morning following their last business meeting, he wasn't sure if God wanted him to bet everything on the stock or merely buy a membership for $9 a month, and being now wealthy and leaning conservative in nature, he had opted for the latter. Still, he had been going to movies at least twice a week, all for the grand price of $9 a month and he'd miss the bargain. In spite of this, once Proposition Paulie thought about it for a while, he concluded that if he now had to pay $9 every time he went to a movie, it wouldn't change his life an iota, and as he said to himself, "Under the circumstances, if life is like a street, I guess I'm still better being on this side of the road rather than across.", both starting and ending the same sentence with a preposition. Mrs. Whibble would have been incredibly proud.

Chapter Four

The Baker's Dilemma

S hmuley's world was a compendium of dilemmas from as early as he could remember.

He was born Shmuel (Samuel) but from the outset nobody called him Shmuel. All his birth documentation, school reports, government forms, tax returns, credit cards, receipts, or anything else that required proof of birth or verification of existence identified him as Shmuel. But from the moment after his father and mother determined he would bear the given name of his late grandfather, nobody, including his parents ever called him anything but Shmuley.

Shmuley was strong as a bull and sharp as a scythe, or so declared his teachers. Having been born and raised in the Bronx, however, he had never seen a bull nor a scythe, so this was the second of the many dilemmas that followed him around like his faithful dog Dawg. His folks had bought Dawg for him when he was just two years old and to ensure that he understood it was his responsibility to look after the animal, had permitted him naming rights. At that point in his life, Shmuley wasn't the most talkative of lads so when his folks demanded for the first, second and fiftieth time what he wished to name his dog, each time he responded with 'Dawg'. So Dawg it was. The dilemma arose from the fact that when some kid bigger than him demanded to know the name of his dog, and Shmuley responded with 'Dawg', like the inquiry wasn't worthy of a serious answer, this generally led to a confrontation of one kind or another, and he might have had better luck had he just named his dog 'go fuck yourself'.

Shmuley was a baker like his father before him. Much of his strength was derived from having worked in his father's bakery as a young boy shlepping 50-pound bags of flour the way most kids would carry bags of potato chips. Shmuley never considered becoming a professional of any kind or pursuing an advanced education. His older brother had become a successful chartered accountant which meant it was bashert (destined) that Shmuley being the only other child should take over the family business which he did. And built it into the largest, best known, and iconic of all the bakeries in the five Burroughs. As the joke went, you could die for his blintzes, knishes, kugels, varenikes and hamantaschen, and if you consumed enough, you probably would.

Shmuley's third dilemmas was of course the baker's dozen. Tradition, as well as every Jewish baba who visited his store demanded that when they ordered a dozen of anything they should receive a baker's dozen i.e. thirteen. This wasn't a problem, since Shmuley was incredibly generous and would offer free samples of everything to everyone and without even thinking would always add a little extra something to everybody's order. The dilemma arose whenever during a conversation somebody would say "It's six of one, half dozen of another" since being a baker, this meant "six of one, six and a half of another" which made no sense, but since Shmuley was gentle as a lamb, although strong as a bull, he avoided confrontation of any kind and was constrained from correcting the offending homily, which only served to aggravate the ulcer he had developed from taste testing everything he baked.

All of which led to Shmuley's great confrontation. Of all the various incredible noshes for which Shmuley was famous, his best known and best loved was his egg custard tarts, a flaky dough filled with an incredible custard, the recipe for which was known only to Shmuley and his father before him. Shmuley would come to the bakery early in the morning and lock himself in the back room where he would prepare the custard. Nobody was allowed into the room during these preparations since the recipe was as closely guarded as the Coke formula. Other bakeries tried to duplicate it, but none could. People who moved from the Bronx to the other coast would still fly in boxes of Shmuley's egg custard tarts for special occasions like weddings or Bar Mitzvahs, or for no other reason than to impress their friends with some taste delight which they could never find elsewhere or replicate.

It was on a late Friday afternoon in early May. Shmuley was preparing to close the store for Shabbat (the Sabbath), not to reopen until Sunday morning which was the tradition his father had begun some seventy years earlier. As he was preparing to turn out the lights, there was a knocking at the front door and Shmuley came out of the back to find Artie Shane banging incessantly on the glass. Artie Shane had been born Arthur Schmelnitsky but had changed it early on in his business career having decided that an Art Shane could advance more quickly in the WASP environment that he hoped to dominate than could an Artie Shmelnitsky.

Shmuley opened the door to explain to Artie that he was closed for the evening but before he could say anything, Artie in his usual fashion pushed Shmuley aside and barged into the store and began examining all the pastries in the display cases. Ignoring Shmuley's protestations that the store was closed for the day, Artie confronted Shmuley in the manner some asshole might adopt with somebody who had dared to suggest to his spoiled cretin of an offspring that it wasn't polite to pee in the corner of your store and demanded to know where the egg custard tarts were.

Patiently, although anxious to get home and wanting to tell Artie to just go fuck himself, Shmuley explained that they had run out of egg custard tarts and unfortunately, there wouldn't be more until Sunday.

Without missing a beat, Artie responded with "Don't tell me that somebody with your gut isn't taking home three dozen for the weekend. All I want is six. I'm having a couple of friends for dinner, and they explicitly asked for your egg custard tarts." Punctuating these comments with several pokes in Shmuley's gut, he added "A guy like you, three dozen or two and a half dozen, you'll never get enough, so what's the difference? Six of one, half dozen of the other."

Shmuley just smiled and said "I was taking two dozen home for my family, but I guess I can spare six. I'll get the box."

Shmuley proceeded to the back and brought the two boxes of his tarts to the front together with a smaller box to hold the six for Artie. He opened both of his two boxes on the counter and then opened the smaller box for Artie and turned to him and asked "I have a dozen of the chocolate and a dozen of the banana. Would you prefer six of one or a mixture?"

Rather than responding as a normal human being might and saying "That's very thoughtful of you. Thanks but just give me whatever you prefer.", Artie laughed and once again poking Shmuley in the stomach said "Did I call it, or did I call it? Fat guys like you, there's no way you're not taking home a couple of dozen. And really, if you have eighteen or twenty-four, you'll probably finish most of them off before you even get home so what's the difference. Like I said, six of one, half dozen of the other."

Now this may have been the six hundredth or seven hundredth time Shmuley had heard that saying, but the number really didn't matter. It was just one time too many, having to smile and say nothing. Shmuley smiled at Artie and said "Actually that might be true if you were speaking to anyone but a baker. But for bakers, there is a difference. For us, that means six of one, six and a half of the other. You know, the 'baker's dozen'".

Artie stared at him for perhaps thirty seconds and then said, "And I give a fuck why"?

Shmuley smiled, grabbed Artie by the neck using only one of his huge paws and walked him over to the counter where the open boxes were waiting, stood him in front of the counter with one hand still wrapped around his neck and said "You should give a fuck because it means you have to eat six and a half rather than just six. Open your mouth."

And he squeezed Artie's neck until his mouth flapped open and then shoved one of the custard tarts into Artie's mouth and said "Eat it. You're not going anywhere until you've finished."

Once Artie swallowed the tart, Shmuley repeated the process until he had finished six of them. Then with one hand still around Artie's neck, Shmuley broke one of the remaining six in the box in half and pushed it into Artie's mouth.

Once this was done, Shmuley said "On second thought, there are only five and a half left in the box, so you might as well have these too." He then proceeded to rub the remaining five and a half tarts all over Artie's face and hair and with crumbs and custard littering Artie's entire head, Shmuley frog marched him to and then out of the door, slamming it behind him.

Artie made his way home to find one of his dinner guests, Sherman Planz, a friend as well as a criminal attorney standing on the steps waiting for him. Artie explained what had transpired and demanded that Sherman arrange to have charges filed against Shmuley. Between unrestrained laughter, Sherman explained that the chances of putting together a jury of twelve people in the Bronx without at least one person who hated Artie or worse, with less than six of whom weren't devotees of Shmuley's egg custard tarts or huge fans of Shmuley himself was equivalent to a moon landing using Sherman's stomach gas as the rocket propellant.

Over the next several days, Sherman told the story to six of his closest friends, who told it to six of their closest friends and within a week the story had spread from the Bronx to at least three of the other four Burroughs and had quickly become known simply as *Custard's Last Stand*.

Chapter Five

Send in the Clowns

Dubikoff wasn't oblivious to the fact that his fear of clowns was irrational. Truth be told, one of the reasons he had obtained his PhD at Cornell on the phobia of clown's aka coulrophobia was to try and deal with this fear without the embarrassment of seeking professional help, since his mother had always told him, "You're not crazy. Clowns are creepy. Those big noses, colored faces, funny clothes." Mind you, that was her go to explanation for her disdain for Jews, and with variations, Blacks, Hispanics, Muslims, and most other people she didn't like.

It's quite possible that Dubikoff could have led a relatively normal life, but for Steven Sondheim and Judy Collins. The first time he heard *Send In the Clowns* by Judy Collins in 1977 was the last time he was able to enjoy a good night's sleep, since after nodding off for a couple of hours, he would hear the song in his head, know the clowns were coming for him, and by the time he heard the line *"Don't bother they're here."* well that's all she wrote, and he was up and awake for the rest of the night.

Notwithstanding the song, with the shutdown of most circuses across the country, Dubikoff might still have led a relatively normal life, at least normal for Dubikoff. He went on to marry, had two kids, and a decent job, at least until Tyler Worthington the third came on the scene.

Tyler Worthington the first made his money the old-fashioned way, destroying the environment and taking advantage of migrant labor in the oil fields of Texas. His son, Tyler Worthington the second, was a remittance man, having moved to Los Angeles, graduated from UCLA with a degree in something incapable of producing any income, and then was satisfied to settle down in Beverly Hills with his trophy wife, trust fund remittances, and golf club membership.

Which brings us to Tyler Worthington the third, or Ty as his parents called him. It was Ty's fifth birthday and he made it clear to his parents that he wanted a birthday party with all his friends who would bring him magnificent presents. Also, for his birthday party as entertainment, he wanted clowns.

As with many Los Angeles parents, for important events such as weddings, Bar Mitzvahs, and fifth birthdays, cost was no consideration, so Tyler the second engaged an agency to locate twelve of the best surviving clowns and one of the legendary clown cars, and to bring them into Los Angeles for young Ty's party. The plan was that at exactly noon, the clown car would roll up to the house, mid party, and the twelve clowns would exit the car and proceed to entertain the privileged children with hilarious things such as squirting each other with seltzer bottles.

Tyler the second was paying a fee of one hundred thousand dollars for these gentlemen, not a penny too much to see the smile on Young Ty the third's face, so the day before the event, after the rehearsal, the assembled clowns decided they should celebrate, what with this being their first paid event in almost a decade, and also being the biggest payday they had ever received. That evening they went on a tour of L.A.'s finest drinking establishments, which tour ended around three the next morning.

Unfortunately, being older gentlemen, and not used to the quality or quantity of spirits consumed the evening before, most of them slept in the next morning, and then, somewhat dazed, nauseous, and a bit bewildered, they didn't assemble to depart for the event until 11:15. Undeterred, the Squirty Dozen climbed into the clown car and set off for Beverly Hills.

Which brings us back to Dubikoff. It was 11:40 a.m., and Dubikoff was heading to Melrose Avenue to meet with a client. As he entered Melrose, the clown car was heading in the opposite direction on the four-mile journey to Beverly Hills. Regrettably, they were behind schedule, driving fast and erratically, and one of the older clowns who had imbibed much more than he should have the night before began to get woozy and then threw up on the adjacent clown. This set of a chain of vomiting which finally reached the driver, who attempting to avoid the deluge, unintentionally swerved the car and swiped Dubikiff's car approaching from the opposite direction.

Both cars stopped and Dubikoff exited his vehicle, intending to exchange particulars with the driver of the other vehicle. It was at this point that the twelve clowns proceeded to exit their car, one by one, most of them still heaving. Dubikoff took one look and then proceeded to run down Melrose screaming, "They're here, they're here. They're taking over the world and they're going to kill us."

Sadly, the story doesn't end here. Dubikoff was institutionalized for six years, until finally, on July 3rd, 2016, he was deemed fit to re-enter society. On the morning of July 4th, Dubikoff's wife attended the institution and took him home. It was noon and he was relaxing on the couch, enjoying a sandwich, coffee, and cake his wife had made for him to celebrate his return. Having been absent from society since 2010, Dubikoff decided it was time to find out what was happening in the world, so he switched on CNN, and the first thing he heard was "Ladies and Gentlemen, the President of the United States" and then the camera focused on a large man with straw hair, an orange face, a foolish smile, and a red tie hanging down to his knees.

Dubikoff has been institutionalized since, and the only words he's been heard to utter are, "Don't bother, they're here."

Chapter Six

Me and the Kernel

It was September 19th, 1995, and an announcement had just come over the news that Orville Redenbacher had passed away. Within the hour, I had faxed a submission to *Saturday Night Live* for a proposed sketch as follows:

The setting – Final Rest Funeral Chapel and Crematorium

An extremely large crowd is gathered. At the front of the room, a solemn faced Pastor addresses the crowd while two attendants stand, one on each side, beside a rolling gurney on which rests an ornate casket.

Pastor – "My dear friends. We are gathered here this afternoon to pay our final tributes and respects to our dear friend Orville Redenbacher whose soul has now departed from this mortal coil to join his maker.

The attendants open the door to the crematorium and roll the gurney to the opening and respectfully lift the casket on to the slide of rollers that will take the casket to its ultimate destination where it will be transposed by the fire from a casket and a body into ashes.

Pastor (continues) — "As will all of us, and as it is written in the good book, we are created from ashes, and we return to ashes. Ashes to ashes, dust to dust. But we do not mourn the passing of our brother Orville Redenbacher, for surely, as his mortal remains are committed to fire and return to ashes from whence they came, I can only remind you that"

From inside the crematorium ovens, the sound begins

Pop,,,,Pop....Pop...Pop...Pop Pop Pop Pop Pop

I never heard back from Saturday Night Live, and the sketch was never performed.
What? Too soon

Chapter Seven

Gus and The Hurricane

Other than being vertically challenged Gus, one of my oldest friends, was remarkably content. He was vertically challenged in that his growth spurt has stopped shortly after it began at 5'4". Being a huge sports fan, this had been disappointing for Gus's athletic aspirations, but other than that, he never allowed it to interfere with his life.

Trained by his father who was a stockbroker and financial genius, Gus followed in his father's also somewhat diminutive footsteps and acquired significant wealth. He had a beautiful penthouse on Western Avenue in Seattle, overlooking the water and not far from the *Pike Place Market*. Gus was intelligent, funny, quite charming, wealthy, and, as a bonus, played piano and sang, both quite credibly, so he was never at a loss for social companionship. In fact, he was constantly pursued by many highly desirable professional women, doctors, lawyers, accountants, and businesswomen. The problem was that Gus enjoyed his single lifestyle and only had interest in women in the other profession, the ones who would leave him to his peace and quiet an hour or so after they arrived.

It was on Gus's sixtieth birthday that he met The Hurricane. He had been celebrating his birthday with myself and a few other friends at *Martin's off Madison* when he had passed the bar and had seen The Hurricane. She was Asian, petite, quite beautiful, and Gus was immediately intrigued. Once he determined that she was there in her professional capacity, he was in love.

Their relationship continued thereafter, hot, and heavy. If The Hurricane had awarded frequent flyer points, Gus would have been eligible for numerous around the world adventures, speaking both literally and figuratively. On the first anniversary of their meeting, they were back at Gus's penthouse when he suggested that perhaps she should cease her professional life and move in with him. The Hurricane lost it. She began accusing Gus of being possessive, controlling and manipulative, all the while punctuating her remarks by throwing pieces of Gus's Waterford crystal and Limoges's vases in his direction. The next day, after Gus had related the incident to me, I dubbed Katrina, her real name, as The Hurricane, which because of her mercurial temperament, stuck.

They carried on their somewhat unusual and stormy relationship for six years. Then on their sixth anniversary, The Hurricane announced that the relationship wasn't healthy for either of them and she was moving to Chicago. She could not be deterred, and much to Gus's despair, she left. They continued to communicate via phone and email for much of the next year, but that was the extent of it. Then, two weeks before his sixty-seventh birthday, Gus called and attempted to persuade The Hurricane to fly in and celebrate it with him. She relented, and Gus sent her a ticket.

The first two days of her visit went without incident and were thoroughly enjoyable. Then, on the evening of the second day, Gus suffered a major heart attack. He was rushed to the hospital where he remained for the next eighteen hours with The Hurricane beside his bed, holding his hand, until peacefully, he passed away.

The Hurricane remained in Seattle for the next four days, visiting friends, until she was scheduled to return to Chicago. While at the airport, she was checking the Seattle Times online and found Gus's obituary. At the end of the obituary, it invited any friends who wished to leave a message online, to do so. The Hurricane wrote "He was a kind and gentle man, my dearest friend, and I shall always miss him." She then boarded her flight for Chicago.

Once underway, the pilot announced that they were expecting substantial turbulence right through to Chicago where the weather was unsettled and stormy. For some reason however, the flight was calm and without incident, and once over Chicago, it was a clear blue sky, with no wind whatsoever. The Hurricane settled into Chicago peacefully. The pilot suggested that this may have been the result of unexpected trade winds, but I'd like to believe that Gus read The Hurricane's comment and had simply blown all the clouds away.

Chapter Eight

Don't Just Stand There

To make this chapter appear a little more structured and a little less like the disturbed ramblings of an aged and deteriorating mind, let's make believe that we are playing a home game of Improv Comedy. We have asked the audience to suggest three subjects and the suggestions were rock and roll, stand-up comedy, and Nazi Germany.

As an entertainment attorney, much of my practice in the early years revolved around the music industry. Consequently, I was the beneficiary of a multitude of stories true or apocryphal about music icons. One of my favorites involved two industry giants, Little Richard and Jerry Lee Lewis. The story had been related to me by several music cognoscenti, and a version of this was reported at the time by Bill Dahl in the *Chicago Tribune*.[1]

[1.] Bill Dahl, Chicago Tribune, August 28th, 1995

Little Richard and Jerry Lee were engaged as headliners to perform on a double bill. Regrettably, it had never been clarified as to who would be the opener and who would close and neither of the two would agree. No headliner wants to open any event lest the audience assumes that he is just an opening act for the next performer. At the last minute, Little Richard finally relented and agreed to appear on stage first.

As Dahl relates, resplendent in a glittering white suit, Little Richard hopped atop his piano, arms outstretched, before he ever sang a note. Once seated behind the keys, he screamed his rock classics-*Good Golly Miss Molly,""Ready Teddy.""Tutti Frutti," "Lucille,""Long Tall Sally,"* and a truly incendiary rendition of *"Keep a Knockin'"*-as though he were 22 years old instead of 62.

I'm told that he danced, screamed and that he was so fired up that he managed to wring out every bit not only of his own energy but that of the audience as well and then to the massive roar and appreciation of the gathered throngs, he exited the stage. And I was informed that as he passed Jerry Lee standing on the side of the stage, he smiled and said, "Top that, asshole."

According to Dahl, by comparison, the traditionally fire-breathing Lewis at times seemed a bit tame, and despite performing all his classics like *"Roll Over Beethoven'""Whole Lotta Shakin' Going On'"* and his trademark *"Great Balls Of Fire"*, Lewis was never able to recover the audience's enthusiasm or participation and, after kicking over his piano bench in his time-honored fashion, exited the stage in disgust.

I have always believed that there is no harder job in the world than that of stand-up comic. You are up there naked, metaphorically speaking, baring your soul in front of an audience, knowing you have nowhere to go if you fail to connect. You do whatever you can to win them over with your best material, but it's a struggle. If you fail, there's nowhere to hide. Persevere, or die. And most stand-up comics may have to hang in for five years or more before they can count on a friendly reception. I could never understand what possibly motivated them.

A few years back, an old and dear friend of mine decided to celebrate his eightieth birthday by holding a party in Los Angeles for three hundred of his closest friends aboard a chartered boat sailing from Marina del Rey. Had he invited all his friends, there would have been a thousand guests, but the main dining room on the ship could only accommodate three hundred so the party was restricted to only his closest friends. Because his friends included many of entertainment industry's notable names, people like David Steinberg, Allan Blye, Bob Einstein (Super Dave and Curb Your Enthusiasm's Marty Funkhauser), Len Cariou and Norm Crosby, many of the guests were people you might expect to see at some media event. In addition, while strolling around the ship before dinner, enjoying cocktails and hors d'oeuvres, you would overhear conversations among many of the guests talking about their legendary friends, some still with us and some departed, people like Carl and Rob Reiner, Mel Brooks, Sid Caesar, Milton Berle, James Aubrey (former head of CBS) and iconic film director Arthur Hiller. For an outsider such as myself, in many respects it felt like I was attending a retrospective celebration at the Emmy's or Academy Awards.

Initially, the intended master of ceremonies for the evening was Perry Rosemond, a brilliant comedic writer, director, and producer and one of our older friends. At the last minute, Perry had been unable to attend, and my friend asked me to fill in for him. Despite my reluctance to assume this responsibility, when my friend asked there was no way I could refuse.

The main dining room could just accommodate three hundred people seated at round tables of eight seats each, and there was no way it could also hold a head table with a podium. Accordingly, I was seated at one of such tables with my friend and his immediate family in the center of the room. In order that I might have a view of the entire room while performing, I opted to handle the formal part of the evening by standing at one end of the room just in front of the entrance to the room itself, my theory being if things went badly, I could escape easily and swim for shore from wherever in the Pacific we happened to be at the time.

Using just a hand-held mic with no podium and a great deal of trepidation, I began the ceremonies and much to my delight, things moved along swimmingly, in the sense that my monologue and introductions were exceedingly well received by the assembled crowd, not that I had elected to abandon ship and was swimming towards, well you get the picture. Truth be told, I was on a roll and the crowd was laughing and appreciating my efforts.

The third guest I called on to offer his thoughts was our host's friend Mark Schiff, a talented stand-up comic. Mark often opened for Jerry Seinfeld who was purported to have said that "Mark Schiff is the funniest, the brightest, the best stage comic I have ever seen." I introduced Mark and then stood aside to let him address the crowd. He told about a dozen stories and was extremely funny and well received. Finally, he told a variation of an old joke. The original joke tells the story about a Russian nobleman in the 19th century who marries a young woman at a small church in Siberia. After the ceremony and reception, the couple leave the church in his horse drawn sleigh to head home to his estate. After a short while, a train passes by on the tracks near the road and the horse is spooked and begins to buck. The nobleman yanks the reins to stop the horse, then gets down from the sleigh, walks in front of the horse, holds up one finger and says, "That's one." He gets back in the sleigh, and they proceed a little further down the road when a fox bounds from the woods and runs across the road, again causing the horse to become unsettled and buck. Once more, the nobleman yanks the reins bringing the sleigh to a halt, gets out, walks in front of the horse, holds up two fingers and says, "That's two."

He then climbs back in the sleigh, and they proceed on their journey. Shortly thereafter, a sleigh approaches them on the road from the opposite direction. As it passes their sleigh, the horse becomes unsettled once again and starts to buck. The nobleman brings the sleigh to a halt, reaches behind the seat, and removes a shotgun, climbs down, and walks in front of the horse and says, "That's three" and shoots the horse in the head. As the horse collapses dead on the road, the nobleman walks back to the sleigh, replaces the shotgun behind the sleigh and climbs aboard as if nothing had happened. His new bride is apoplectic and says "I can't believe it. You're a monster. If I had known this about you, I would never have agreed to marry you." The nobleman looks at her for about thirty seconds, pauses, and then holding up one finger says, "That's one."

Now as I said, he told a variation of this story, but I don't recall the details, since I was standing there watching him take control of the audience, I had worked so hard to make my own and with whom I would now be back to square one. As he finished his version of the story with, "That's one", and the crowd who obviously had never heard the story before broke into unrestrained laughter, like the professional he was he knew to leave when he was on a high. He smiled at the crowd, nodded, turned with his back to the crowd and handed the mic back to me, at the same time smiling with a look that I knew, without him saying anything, was a kinder version of what Little Richard had muttered to Jerry Lee, namely "Top that, asshole."

I took the mic as he casually strolled back to his table, and said, "Thank you Mark. You were superb. I had the crowd in the palm of my hand until your performance, but somehow you managed to steal them from me and kill my momentum." Then I held up one finger and said, "That's one." It brought down the house and suddenly I realized why stand-up comics do it. There is nothing in the world like the rush you get when you adlib, score, and the audience is there for you.

I have a dear friend, Frannie Sheridan, an international performer, writer, and comedienne who lives in Florida. She also has a hugely successful podcast, and she and her husband Dani operate an amazing Wellness Center in West Palm Beach.

Frannie's parents were Holocaust survivors whom upon their arrival in North America in the 1940's were greeted by several anti Semitic experiences. As a result, Frannie's father elected to change his name to Sheridan and try and pass as Irish Catholic. He went so far as to enroll Frannie in a Catholic girl's school. The problem was Frannie's Jewish genes were too strong and she stood out like schmaltz herring in a lemon meringue pie. Ultimately, she reverted to her Jewish heritage. Frannie wrote a stage play about her family which was met with great acclaim and attracted the attention of Arthur Hiller who became her friend and mentor. Several years ago, Frannie approached me to help her write a screenplay based on her play, which we did, titled *Dancing on Hitler's Grave*. I also offered some small assistance on her autobiography *Confessions of a Jewish Shiksa*.

Over the past decade, I have written material for Frannie's stand-up appearances. One of the jokes I wrote was about two old Jews huddled together in a cattle car along with several hundred others on a train heading to a German concentration camp during World War 11. One of the old fellows turns to the other and says, "I guess business class was full." Now as I mentioned earlier, one of the reasons Jews have been able to survive over the millennia has been their ability to laugh at themselves, no matter how desperate their situation. Knowing this, I was still reluctant to give Frannie this joke because of her family's background. I finally relented and sent it to her and not missing a beat, she used it in a performance before a large audience, many of them older Jews. And they loved it.

Frannie has incredible courage. I could write that joke but there is no way I could ever have delivered it. Which is why I am content to hide behind my pen. Sometimes I even require an imaginary game of Improv Comedy just to tell a personal story.

Chapter Nine

David Steinberg, J.R. Tolkien, and Me

Helen Hunt tried to get me into bed with her.

Perhaps I'm getting ahead of myself. No doubt you've heard of the theory of six degrees of separation. Stated simply, it contends that nobody in the world is separated by more than six levels of people. In other words, everyone you know is the first level, i.e. perhaps a thousand people. Everyone those thousand people know are the second level and so on. By the time you reach the sixth level of separation, statistically speaking, it is impossible that you wouldn't have covered every living person in the world. The variation on the theme that was making the rounds related to one of the Kevin's (Bacon, Spacey or Costner, although I believe it was the former). In any event, the theory was that if you took all the people who had appeared in old Kev's movies, together they would have appeared in movies with every actor in the business today, or some such silliness.

Many years ago, when I was still married, my wife and I went to see a Kevin Costner movie, but it was sold out. So, we went instead to one starring Helen Hunt, who at one point in the film appeared nude. And certainly, appeared none the worse for it. That night, I dreamt about Helen Hunt. We were at a cocktail party at David Steinberg's house, whom I grew up with. (David Steinberg, not his house). As children growing up, David and I had been friends. In fact, we both dated the same girl, although at different times. She ultimately left our hometown to study in England and ended up marrying J.R. Tolkien's son. David left for Hollywood. And I stayed behind to contemplate their success. Among his other accomplishments, David was Helen Hunt's director in her TV sitcom *Mad About You*, which of course is the first degree of separation and why the cocktail party in my dream was at his house.

Everyone at the party was dressed in their finest, except for Helen Hunt who was nude. Or dressed in her finest, depending on your point of view. In any event, she approached me and asked if I would be interested in going to bed with her. I seem to recall her saying something about being fascinated by short, fat, older Jewish men, but that may just have been my subconscious rationalizing. I explained that I was happily married and devoted to my wife. She seemed somewhat hurt, but accepting the inevitable, moved on to proposition her second choice, Kevin Bacon.

Aside from permitting me the opportunity of dropping David Steinberg and J.R. Tolkien's names, I have written this with a further purpose. On the chance that Helen Hunt should ever read this, I want her to know that we do things a little differently in this neck of the woods. It may be okay in Hollywood circles to come on brazenly as she did, but quite frankly, here in the boondocks, this just isn't acceptable. If she was sincere in her offer, she would have been much better received had she not approached me while I was standing next to my wife. In the great Northwest, we still understand the meaning of gallantry.

Chapter Ten

The Day the Rains Came

If you had to retire, there were certainly many worse places to do so than Poipu Beach, Kauai. Kauai, home of the movies *South Pacific* and *Jurassic Park* was called the Garden Isle because of the lush vegetation. With all the rain the island received, it would have been difficult for anything not to grow. Ostensibly, there were parts of Kauai that received more rain annually than any other place on the planet. Fortunately, because of the trade winds, Poipu Beach was generally sunny, other than in the rainy season when the rains came like clockwork. Setting that aside, however, for all the other seasons, if you had to retire, and were looking to do it in a less than visible place, Poipu Beach was ideal. And this was the rainy season so, most of the time, Sebastian could be found at home in his condo.

Sebastian had to retire. He was forty-seven, which might not seem old to many, but in Sebastian's profession, forty-seven was ancient. Sebastian was a hired assassin and had been since the age of eighteen. Twenty-nine years was a long run in that business, and all things considered, Sebastian had seen no point in trying to extend it to thirty.

Sebastian's mistake had been in allowing his sense of humor to rule his better judgment. It was a general rule in the circles in which Sebastian ran that you never kill the messenger, because it was nothing personal and good assassins were hard to find. So Mob A might decide they needed to outsource a hit on a member of Mob B. The hitman was just the messenger, and any retaliation would take place against Mob A, not the hitman. There were even instances where the hitman was retained to look after the retaliation. Those instances were few and far between, but like an attorney hired to look after both sides of a land deal, vendor, and purchaser, they were highly desirable, since from a practical point of view, you were like a farmer, growing your own food.

The hit that had created a 'situation' for Sebastian arose from an engagement he had accepted from Gershon "The Duck" Ziegler, head of the Israeli mafia in New York. There were two schools of thought as to the derivation of The Duck's nickname. The first and most obvious was that he had been born with webbed toes, which was true, he had. There was a second school of thought however, that the name was derived from the fact that shortly after he had ascended to power, he had personally terminated his predecessor Izzie "the gimp" Feldstein, whose nickname was derived from his wooden leg, occasioned by an injury received during the Six-Day War. Utilizing a woodchipper, The Duck had reduced Izzie to wood chips and other less biodegradable substances, and then in a moment of sentimentality he had ordered the resulting detritus be thrown into the duck pond in Central Park, where Izzie used to like to enjoy his noon meal.

Gershon had been training his younger brother Chad to ultimately take over from him when the time came and had dispatched Chad to look after the organizations interests in Miami, all which Chad had been attending to with due diligence. Sadly, he had also been attending to the girl friend of the head of the Russian mafia in New York. Respecting his wife, the Russian kept his girl friend in a condo in Miami and visited her perhaps once a month when looking after his organization's real estate holdings in Miami. The rest of the time she enjoyed the sun, the fine food only to be found in Miami, and the attentions of Chad. The Russian felt that the matter was better handled by outsourcing, so Sebastian had been retained to deal with Chad. Although it wasn't a specific direction, the Russian had indicated a desire that Chad's elimination, if possible, should look like an accident to preclude any retaliation from The Duck.

There were several ways Sebastian could have handled it, a hit and run, an impersonal mugging or robbery gone bad, or any number of other tools in his arsenal. Unfortunately, the temptation was too great, and Sebastian was unable to resist. He had waited in Chad's condo for him to return from what being a vegetarian and lover of salads Chad liked to think of as his Russian Undressing. Sebastian quickly rendered Chad unconscious, and then he created a scenario that made it appear that Chad had been engaged in an attempt at autoeroticism, strangling himself while masturbating, but it had gone wrong, and he had died.

The coroner wasn't fooled, and it was quickly determined that Chad had been murdered. There would have been no retribution, at least as against Sebastian, were it not for the fact that the national papers quickly picked up the story and the headlines became "Miami's last hanging Chad", exactly the thought that had tickled Sebastian's fancy. Nothing could mollify The Duck. Sebastian had broken the rules and caused untold humiliation to The Duck and his family, which could only be satisfied by Sebastian's death, and so a million-dollar contract on Sebastian had been issued, and Sebastian had determined it was time to retire.

There was no reason whatsoever for Sebastian to be cautious or to fail to answer the door for the elderly couple he observed through the spy hole in the door. Jehovah's Witnesses were common in Poipu Beach, often setting up stands in the charming neighboring *Kukui 'ula Shopping Center*. Nowhere was it written that you couldn't spread the word in what to most was already considered paradise.

When they ultimately found Sebastian, it was only because the air conditioning in his unit had gone on the fritz, and he had mildewed sufficiently to attract the attention of several of the other occupants in the building. When the police arrived and managed to enter his suite, they found Sebastian on his bed, on his back, lying there peacefully with his arms crossed over his stomach. In his hands he was holding an issue of

Awake, which the police found somewhat amusing since he was anything but. And it would have been more than surprising if he had been, what with the bullet hole in the middle of his forehead. When the story made the national news, that Sebastian "The Exterminator" Stelter had been exterminated, The Duck was more than exhilarated. He had been assured by his hired assassins that the job had been completed, but until he had the public confirmation, he was seriously on edge. He was also absolutely delighted with the comic touch of the *Awake* magazine. He had been given no idea of how his assassins planned on approaching Sebastian and what form of cover they might use. Nonetheless, they were known for their ingenuity and their sense of humor which was the principal reason The Duck had hired Jason and Martha Rain in the first place.

Chapter Eleven

Cohabitation Is a Four-Letter Word

Once I moved into the bottom half of life's seventh inning, I found that I could no longer be away from the peaceful tranquility of my condo, what I think of as my Fortress of Solitude, for more than two days at a time. If I'm gone for more than that, I begin to lose strength, as if someone had slipped a hunk of Kryptonite into my back pocket of which iniquity, I was blissfully unaware.

I live alone.

Now before you get all sympathetic and cloying, I live alone by choice. I have several good friends I will choose to have lunch with on occasion. I have had numerous relationships. I was married for 25 years. I have three wonderful, incredibly bright, funny, and social sons whom I love dearly and whom I believe kind of like me. So I am neither a hermit nor an outcast. I live alone because I choose to live alone.

I live in the Pacific Northwest. Right next to the ocean. Not in California where the rest of the world lives but further north near the Canadian border where you won't find snakes or almost anything else that crawl on the ground like stealth terrorists or try to bite your ass and infect you with some incurable disease. And no I'm not a hypochondriac. Okay I am a hypochondriac but that's beside the point. You can be a hypochondriac and still cautiously realistic.

I tell you all this so that you will understand that when I say I live alone you will appreciate that my doing so is not only a lifestyle choice, but an incredibly well considered and highly intelligent one.

Once a year, I go to the beautiful ocean adjacent town of Marion Massachusetts to visit my sister at her summer home. Now to my way of thinking, calling this a summer home is like calling the White House a government office. Her 'summer home' is around a hundred thousand square feet (okay maybe just five thousand square feet but when you live in a condo that's 800 square feet, well you get the idea), is located on and looks out over a bay with a vista in either direction of at least two miles. Boats (and yes calling them boats is like calling Neil Armstrong a pilot) bob in the water on the periphery from right to left, or if like me you are left-handed, from left to right. Sailboats, cigarette boats (I always thought these were boats that emitted a great deal of smoke until I started reading spy novels and learned they were high speed boats often used for smuggling drugs), yachts that sleep two to twenty guests, depending on how many other pretentious people you know, and boats with what I am told are flying bridges though to be totally honest I never once saw them take flight.

Where was I? Oh yes, once a year I fly three thousand miles cross country, notwithstanding that I hate flying, to visit my sister whom I love dearly, even more than I hate flying. If God had intended that I should fly, I would have been born a hummingbird. She and her husband live in this modest wannabe Kennedy compound outside of Marion where my guest suite makes my condo look like servants quarters, their screened in porch where I am currently writing this is large enough to have its own zip code, but again you get the idea, and numerous assorted other guest areas, living rooms, dens and rooms nobody ever enters. The porch seats about six hundred, looks over the water and the sculpted lawn between the house and the water and somehow attracts just enough breeze that you're never unduly bothered by what the less civilized urban dwellers might call sweat.

As I said, I love my sister. And should you wonder how much I love her, when I am back home, I walk three hours every day, usually beside the ocean. This is called minimum exercise for old, fat men who don't like real exercise but like the thought of dying less. Accordingly when I visit my sister, I also walk three hours a day through the beautiful surrounding wooded paths and forestry. Prior to leaving the estate each morning, (yes, they all call it 'the estate' rather than 'the house'), it's necessary to take what local people call minimal preparations. You see, there are ticks. I always thought ticks were just something that hillbillies bought when they went to the movies to see Fast and Furious 43 (Give me two of them ticks for me and the missus) but no, these are creepy, crawly little motherfuckers that will attach themselves to parts of your body like barnacles to the underside of a boat (another bit of aquatic knowledge I acquired on one of my earlier visits. Until that time, I had always assumed barnacles were baby Jewish barns.)

Now you will remember that I choose to live in the part of the Pacific Northwest where there are no snakes or other creepy crawly things, not because I have anything against other life forms (at one point in time, I used to like the music of Black Sabbath) but because creepy crawly things scare the shit out of me, whereas in the world of people who live on these estates, these are just a minor inconvenience, notwithstanding that they can infect your body and leave your brain with less active cognitive functions than the mice that discovered and ingested Willie Nelson's hidden cache of weed. So when you prepare to leave the estate for a walk, you first spray every part of your body with Rotting Rats 100 strength tick spray, a solution that smells and feels just like what it's named after. Then after you've completed this ritual, you tuck your pant legs into your socks to ensure the little motherfuckers don't crawl up your shoes and onto your legs where they will slowly creep up and permanently attach themselves to your balls where they won't be found until it's way too late, since at my age nobody, especially me, ever goes near my balls.

Did I mention the whatever's? Little, black, flying turd balls that dive bomb your face while you walk. I've asked numerous native estate residents what these Kamikaze creatures are but the only answer I was ever able to elicit was 'whatever'.

Once I return from my walk, I get to spend the balance of my day with my sister, whom as I said I adore and her husband, who is a lovely man but generally seems angry at the world. He isn't, but grew up in New York, which is usually enough to instil the basic survival knowledge that to persevere and succeed you need not only be cautious, but you should also be aggressive and angry, or all the crazies out there will assume you're a wuss and overwhelm you. He adores my sister, I believe likes me, and is kind, generous and attentive. His demeanour in no way bothers my sister since she is the smartest person I've ever known and tunes out anything she doesn't wish to hear. I, on the other hand, having been a lawyer most of my life, hate contention and hear everything. So what would pass as normal conversation in my sister's house, or probably in any other married couple's house, always sounds like the Ayatollah Khomeini and the head of Israel's Mossad unexpectedly bumping into one another in a hidden underground tunnel.

Did I mention my niece? She generally visits the same time I do and occupies another one of the other large guest wings. She is brilliant, runs one of the country's largest University's, and I love her dearly. Unlike my own children whom, for some reason, didn't inherit the 'cohabitation is a four-letter word' gene, my niece did. So she will spend much of her visit either sleeping, working remotely on her laptop, or exchanging "can you fucking believe this" glances with me when the old good-natured carping begins. She lives alone, happily, enjoys friends when she feels like it, and once a month when I drive into Seattle, joins me for lunch where we briefly update one another on what is happening in our respective world of couples are walking pejoratives.

Most people visiting the estate would consider the week tantamount to an expense free vacation to a world class resort. But most people, unlike myself and my niece don't believe that 'cohabitation' is a four-letter word. Once I board my return flight, manage to arrive home safely, and ensconced in my 800 square feet of quiet paradise, free from interaction with 'people', I am for at least the next 51 weeks, at peace with the world. Or at least until I summon the courage to examine my balls to determine if I brought home any other estate guests with me.

Chapter Twelve

Tut-Tut

While ambling down Washington Blvd. towards Venice Beach recently, when I wasn't sidestepping or tripping over the for-rent battery powered scooters that proliferated the walking areas like hookers in the Garment District, I was captivated by the banners every few feet advertising the 100th anniversary year long exhibition of *King Tut's Treasures of the Golden Pharaoh* at L.A.'s *California Science Center*.

According to a 2014 Gallup poll, four out of ten Americans believe God created humans in their present form some 6,000 year ago. Most of the rest of the people believe in evolution. Regardless of which side of the creationism-evolution argument you may fall on, all agree that humans in their present form existed 6,000 years ago.

For many years, pyramids were the largest structures on earth, and although most were many thousands of years old, before any science of construction had been developed, it is agreed that most involved mathematical and construction details that boggle the imagination of present-day architects. In fact, many of the pyramids embody most of the present-day mathematical formulae regardless of whether they are in Egypt, Mexico, Greece, Sudan, Nigeria, Spain, China, or Peru.

We continue to be confounded by how our ancestors thousands of years ago could create structures with the design, integrity and durability that baffle archaeologists, scientists, and astronomers to this day, such as:

- Three pyramids, Khyfer, Khafre and Menkauree are so perfectly aligned with the stars that they form the constellation of Orion's belt.
- The interior temperature of the Egyptian pyramids always stays constant, and it is always around 20 degrees Celsius, consistent with the average temperature of the earth.
- The Great North Pyramid is the most accurately aligned structure in existence and faces true north with only $3/60^{th}$ of a degree of error, which slight error may be explained by the shift of the North Pole over time.
- The relationship between Pi(p) and Phi(f) is expressed in the fundamental proportions of the Great Pyramid of Giza.
- The curvature designed into the faces of the Great Pyramid of Giza exactly matches the radius of the earth; and

- The Great Pyramid of Giza is exactly equidistant
between the North and South Poles.

Equally confounding is the fact that there are pyramids in
different countries all over the planet, built during a time
when there was no such thing as international travel or
communication and yet strikingly similar in design and date
of construction. How do a dozen similar structures appear in
a dozen different area codes, often thousands of miles apart
without any apparent contact between the various people?

How they managed to emerge in all these diverse
locations sometimes simultaneously has long intrigued me.
I have finally come to what I consider to be the only logical
conclusion.

The Planet Xngpilz (in a galaxy several billion-light years
away).

5,600 B.C.

A group of the planet's leading astrophysicists are seated
in a boardroom. They are conversing in Xngpilzian, which
for purposes of clarity, I have translated into English.

BRX247 – Are you serious? You want to do the pyramid
experiment on that assemblage of cretins in
the third planet from the sun in the chocolate
bar Galaxy?
BRV29 – It's called the Milky Way Galaxy.

BRX247 – Whatever. How far along are they on the evolutionary scale?

BRV29 – Depends on whom you talk to. Some say tens of thousands of years, others say just 400.

BRX247 – Let me get this straight, we're going to send an expeditionary force to this planet, guide the population in different areas of that planet in the construction of our pyramids, utilizing advanced theories of mathematics and construction, and then just leave them and wait and see what happens?

MDRSF22 – That's pretty much what we've done with other planets in other galaxies.

BRX247 – Yes, but they were much more advanced. To try that with this group borders on what our Supreme Leader would call 'Meshuga" (the word doesn't translate from Xngpilzian to English).

BRX247 – Okay, assuming we go ahead with the experiment, how will we know if it works, if they manage to make the necessary advances and develop their civilization?

PTRV42 – I suggest we use the same standard as we have with the other planets. We'll know they've succeeded once there's the emergence of a Kardashian.

MDRSF22 – What he says makes sense. That generally signifies the start of important scientific advances like being able to stop from being put on hold, bags of popcorn that aren't one-third broken kernels that get stuck in your teeth, selfie sticks and a Roomba that does something other than bang into walls.

BRX247 – I'll agree it should prove interesting, although the cost will be immense. Can you give me any more compelling reason why we should undertake this project?

MDRSD247 – It's three months before the start of football season. What else is there to do?

MDRSF22 - All in favor? Carried.

Chapter Thirteen

A Perfect Match

*A*uthor's note: For those of my readers who are not yet satisfied that their expenditure on this book was justified, throughout this chapter I shall be offering several opportunities whereby you might recover your investment.

Matchmaker, matchmaker, make me a match
Find me a find, catch me a catch.[2]

When I first heard these lyrics from *Fiddler on the Roof*, I was by tradition already aware of the role of the Matchmaker or Shadchan, legendary in the Ashkenazi Jewish society, or of similar services in other cultures, from the Hindu Astrologer to the village priest in Medieval Catholic society. In days of old, where the reputation as well as a key bodily

---

[2] Matchmaker Jerrold Lewis Bock / Sheldon M. Harnbick

membrane of daughters were guarded more jealously than the family's assets, such services were essential. And there probably was never a Jewish or Italian mother who hadn't, at one time or another, uttered the words "Have I got a boy/girl for you."

Having grown up however in a society where if you had any hope of getting lucky, you were obliged to go through the mating dance all by yourself, this meant, at least for me, the following life events:

The blind phone call, glancing at notes I'd made previously to try and sound clever and spontaneous, "Hi, I got your number from my friend Charlie, and I was wondering if you might be interested in going to graduation with me?" ("Do I know you?") "We've never met, but we've often passed in the hall at school and" ("Did I ever indicate any interest in you when we passed?") "Not really, but I'm sure if you got to know me, you'd probably regret having passed up the opportunity and hello, hello".

The cold approach at a bar, "Can I join you" ("Do I look like I'm falling apart?"), "Can I buy you a drink?" ("You probably can but if you think that entitles you to join me, save your money.")

The walk up, "Hi, I realize you don't know me, but I couldn't help but notice you and" ("I'm glad you're observant. Now notice how I'm reaching into my purse for Bear spray which I'll use if you're not gone by the time I take it out.")

The let's go to the next step, "I think it's time we moved our relationship to the next level," ("If the next level is the exit, I couldn't agree more.")

The ambiguous hint, "Were you serious when you said you want me to meet your parents." ("Absolutely, I'd love that. They died three years ago.")

And now, after I've been forced to live through all that, I understand that more than 50% of current relationships begin online. In addition to the huge dating sites, eHarmony, Elite Styles, Our Time, Zoosk and Match, there are literally thousands of dating sites appealing to every segment of society, including Christian, Jewish, Indian, Black, Gay, and Lesbian, Latin, Senior and Single Parent to name just a very few. There is even a dating site for farmers (www. farmersdatingsite.com. where single farmers mingle, or so says the banner on the home page. Where single farmers mingle? Seriously guys, that was the best you could come up with. I have to assume that the slogan "Where single down to earth guys gravitate" was already taken by www. gravediggersdatingsite.com. But whereas the thousands of sites cover almost all possibilities, there are always new opportunities for the entrepreneurial.

$Investment opportunity #1 —www.avoidliketheplague.cloud. This will be a site for the absolute dregs of society, the crème de la crème of losers. To be eligible for membership, applicants will have to check off at a minimum 5 of the following criteria:

__Registered sex offender

__Extra body parts (missing body parts doesn't qualify)

__Former notable in entertainment or media industry

__Former member of the clergy

__If incarcerated, eligible for conjugal visits

__Robo telephone solicitor

__Acknowledged nickname indicative of a weapon or fetish

__Considers Oz a comedy and Orange Is the New Black instructional

__Voted for Sherriff Joe Arpaio

__Dentist

Nor is this the only opportunity. Consider the following:

$$Investment opportunity #2- www.ourshadchan.com. Like the lawyer with no will or the tailor with no suit, who makes matches for the matchmaker? Well this dating site will be the answer to that question. Membership will be restricted to matchmakers. It's understood that female matchmakers outnumber male matchmakers fifty to one, so this site won't be dedicated to arranging marriages as much as to ensuring that male matchmakers get laid a lot.

Regardless of which site you choose to join, the first and most serious obstacle you will have to surmount will be whom you are. Certainly you can fudge the facts insofar as your job, your car, your friends, your pastimes, likes and dislikes or why you still live with your parents, but as with everything else in life, every retailer will tell you the first problem is getting the customer in the door. In your case, that means your picture or video. If you don't appeal to your prospective mate visually, there is no way they are going to read further. Which brings us to

$$$Investment opportunity #3 – www.meandmyotherme.com -A collection of 100,000 stock photos and 30 second videos that you can use instead of your own when posting your biographical information on the dating site. There are numerous stock photo sites, but this will be tailored exclusively for dating, with easy access to whatever photo will best meet the requirements of your intended mate, whether the primary features they may be seeking are beauty, athleticism, intellectualism, foot fetish or deformity. Looking at most couples you know, it should be obvious that physical appearance couldn't have been the determining factor in their relationship. Once given the chance to get to know the other person, most people are prepared to overlook any physical deficiencies. Since your intended mate isn't going to see you until after you've completed the online dating process, you can always explain the difference between the 6'3" avatar with smouldering eyes and dark wavy hair to your actual 5'8" bald self to a mix up at the dating site or merely an example of your incredible, creative sense of humor.

This leaves only the two final hurdles, the first date and closing the deal. Accept as a given that whomever you are meeting, they will have an emergency exit plan much like your own. (The phone call from a friend 10 minutes after they arrive, permitting them to allege an emergency requiring them to leave, a feigned headache or if sufficiently desperate, an epileptic attack.) This can be surmounted by choosing a meeting site where you are assured there is no cell service. (For your own protection, just set the alarm on your phone for 10 minutes after the other person arrives and you can claim the alarm is your ringtone). Having ensured they can't escape, your next goal is to overcome all the misconceptions you've created, the picture, the other minor details such as your unemployment, body odor and limp. All these are surmountable if you remember the person you are meeting has probably lied as much or more than you have. Your sole goal must be distraction, making believe that none of the other persons fabrications matter, at least until your own are forgotten. Once you've done that, your home free. And always remember, no matter how crushing the rejection, you can always go to Walmart, buy some tomato seeds and a trowel, plant the seeds in your back yard or on the boulevard, and then go to www.farmersdatingsite.com. If "*Where single farmers mingle*" was the best they could come up with, trust me, the bar has been set very, very low.

Chapter Fourteen

Beverly's Hills

The hills Beverly was forced to climb over the years defending himself from life's vicissitudes had nothing to do with his given name. Beverly was once a common masculine name, and only fell out of favor for boys with the publication and popularity of the 1904 book *Beverly of Graustark* by George Barr McCutcheon about an American woman named Beverly impersonating her cousin to prevent a villain from taking over his kingdom. The only reason he was given the name was a quirk of fate. His Jewish mother Sophie and English Protestant father Frank had planned on calling him Dwight, but a month before his birth, Sophie's mother Beverly unexpectedly passed away, and in accordance with Jewish tradition, Sophie had asked and Frank had agreed that regardless of their child's sex, it would be named after Sophie's late mother. And since most people had always called him B.K., it had nothing to do with Beverly's travails.

Nor it should be pointed out was Richard Nixon responsible for Beverly's woes, notwithstanding that many attributed the origination of that problem at Tricky Dicks feet. Nixon may have been responsible for many perfidious acts, but in this case, his only sin was popularizing something that had been around for the previous half century.

The initial villain in that denigration of Beverly can be traced back to the start of the 20th century. John was one of the pioneers of car manufacturing in the U.S. With the encouragement of Henry Ford, he set up his wheel company in 1910 based in Windsor, Ontario, just across the river from Detroit. He started with wooden wheels which were state of the art, but these subsequently evolved into wire-spoke wheels and later, steel wheels.

And that's where the problem began. John Kelsey's company, the *Kelsey Wheel Company*, became famous for its wheels, and it was popularly acknowledged that nothing could be more secure than the nuts and bolts used to affix the wheels to the car, which gave rise to the whimsical saying, "tighter than Kelsey's nuts". Over the years, the historical relation to car wheels was forgotten, and by the time Beverly's father Frank Kelsey was born, the nuts had a sole anatomical attribution. Ergo, for much of his early life Beverly Kelsey spent an inordinate amount of time explaining that there was absolutely nothing wrong with his balls. Which of course was only the start of the problem.

Beverly's next hurdle came thanks to America's second largest burger franchise, *Burger King*, also known to most of its fans as BK, coincidentally the same nickname as Beverly's. This was never a problem until Beverly's second year at the university of Washington, when Beverly accepted a blind date with a particularly unpleasant young woman whom he chose not to call for a second date. After waiting for a call for a week, she decided it was time to seek revenge and told anybody who would listen that unlike his namesake, Beverly could never lay claim to possessing a whopper, notwithstanding that they had never progressed to even holding hands on the date. It took less than a day for word to spread across campus that B.K. should never be considered synonymous with a whopper.

From that point, life went downhill.

Beverly graduated with a degree in print advertising just before the explosion of social media rendered print advertising relatively worthless.

Beverly decided he would use his advertising skills that nobody else seemed to want for his own benefit and borrowed funds and acquired a *Blockbuster* franchise.

Beverly was married with children when *Blockbuster* folded, and recognizing that he desperately needed a job, and understanding from watching his own children that the safest job he could find would be with *Toys R Us*, he signed on as an advertising executive.

And then seemingly tired of screwing with Beverly, fate decided to give him a break. In the fall of 2011, Beverly convinced his wife to take $3000.00 of their meager savings to purchase 1500 *Bitcoins* at an average price of $1.50. When *Bitcoin* rose to over $13,000 in 2018, they agreed their worries were over and it was time to cash in. Unfortunately, they were unable to find where Beverley had hidden their 18-figure password that would enable them to access the digital wallet that held their *Bitcoins*, so it appeared that once again the fickle finger of fate had intervened in Beverly's life, inserting one final hill he would be unable to climb.

On September 16th, 2021, no longer able to afford the mortgages on their house, Beverly and his wife sold their home, and prepared to move. While packing, they discovered the copy of *Beverly of Graustark* Beverly had purchased twenty years earlier at a garage sale and in which he had forgotten until then that he had hidden the password to their digital wallet. Two days later they sold their 2000 *Bitcoin* at an average price of $66,000, just weeks before the beginning of the precipitous decline in *Bitcoin*'s value.

Now retired, the Kelsey's are enjoying their new life in their recently acquired home in, where else, Beverly Hills.

Chapter Fifteen

Once Upon a Time in the East

In retrospect, I suppose the ultimate credit should go to *ancestors.com* and *23andme.com*.

Henry McCarty was born in Brooklyn on August 6th, 1996, but was abandoned by his mother shortly thereafter and never got to know her, his father, or any other relatives. The only thing she left him was his name. Understandably, with a rather large chip on his shoulder, Henry moved from foster home to foster home, never lasting more than a few months in one place. The problem wasn't just the mega chip he carried on his shoulder, it was that Henry was fearless, aggressive, and a better street fighter than almost anybody he encountered. And if they were better, he learned from them, and ultimately was in a class by himself. Physically, he was small, but because he had no fear of whatever injuries might befall him, he was virtually unbeatable. You could beat him until the sun came up, but he wouldn't stay down.

Likely, but for the internet, Henry might have ended up in prison or in the morgue before the age of 18. But one day, with nothing else to do, Henry began to stroll through the World Wide Web on an iPhone he had recently stolen. Somewhat curious as to whether he had any relatives on whom he might impose, Henry entered Henry McCarty on *Google* to see what might come up. And what came up was "Billy the Kid, born Henry McCarty in New York City in 1859, also known by the pseudonym William H. Bonney, was an outlaw and gunfighter of the American Old West, and is alleged to have shot and killed 21 men before he himself was killed at the age of 21 by Sherriff Pat Garrett."

Utilizing *23andme.com* and then *ancestors.com*, Henry was ultimately able to determine a direct lineage to his famous ancestor, and that was the beginning of his amazing transformation. Finding that he was unable to convince people of his ties to Billy the Kid using physical force, Henry began to focus his considerable intelligence on enhancing his verbal skills. He became a regular at school, rather than a constant absentee. He studied, he read, and most importantly, he joined the school's debate team where he excelled. There were others with greater knowledge, skill, and experience, but it turned out that nobody had Henry's wit and humor, something which he had acquired in dealing with the hand life had dealt him. Like fat kids who use humor as a defence mechanism, throughout his early years Henry had used humor to confront life rather than succumbing.

All of this might have come to nothing, but for Megan McCarthy, a girl on the debating team Henry began to date.

One day she told him that for her birthday, she wanted to go to a comedy club, and eager to please her, Henry agreed to take her. They were enjoying themselves immensely, until the comic noticed them in the audience, particularly Megan who was very attractive, noticed Henry's diminutive size, and seeking to impress Megan said to her "I see you brought a garden gnome with you. Did they charge you admission for it." There was a day when Henry would have performed a colonoscopy on the comic utilizing his mic stand, but instead, without losing a beat, Henry shouted back "I may be small, but I've taken dumps bigger than you, and looking at you, you may be one of them." This started a back and forth with the comic, and it wasn't a contest. Henry chewed him up and spit him out, and the crowd gave Henry a standing ovation. He was hooked.

In a short time, Henry began attending comedy clubs all around New York, bantering with comics, and very quickly achieved a city-wide reputation as a brilliant comedic mind. Then one day, he was approached by a representative from a major television network who asked Henry if he wanted to develop a show for the network. Only 19, Henry quickly submitted a proposal for a show starring himself. They loved it, and the following September, the show aired.

Henry moved to Los Angeles, bought a 6,000 square foot home in Beverly Hills, and began to live a life he could never have even imagined growing up in Brooklyn. Then after the end of season one, the network announced that they would not be renewing the show for a second season, which meant there wouldn't be the requisite 100 episodes necessary for a lucrative distribution deal and that Henry wouldn't be able to repay the money he had borrowed to purchase his house based on a contemplated five season run and distribution deal. Henry lost it. In a fit of rage Henry went to network headquarters, waving a replica of William Bonney's pistol he had purchased online and threatened to kill everybody if they didn't renew his show for a second season. Unaware that it was just a replica and not loaded, the head of building security Rick "Patrick" Garrett shot and killed Henry. Henry was 21.

Henry was buried in the Forest Lawn Cemetery in Los Angeles. His tombstone reads,

Henry McCarty, aka Billy the Kidder.
1996 - 2017

"Everyone who's ever lived has been the sum of their ancestor's choices. That's the human condition."
Felicity Hayes-McCoy

"The life of the dead is placed in the memory of the living."
Marcus Tullius Cicero

R.I.P.

Chapter Sixteen

I Thought He Was Dead

He was a terrific actor. Not Marlon Brando or Tom Hanks terrific, but still very good. The problem was, to put it kindly, he himself wasn't overly memorable. Not good looking enough to land the lead roles so from the outset he was a character actor. But a very good one. You would probably remember the character; you just wouldn't remember him.

You'd never hear him complain. He was shy and not comfortable around people, so he rarely dated, didn't have more than a few friends, and never married. Financially, he did well, so he was able to acquire a lovely bungalow on Hill St. in Santa Monica with a garden, a sitting area, and a lovely view, all of which he enjoyed immensely.

Nor did he go unrecognized professionally. During his career he was nominated twice for Academy Awards for a supporting role and three times for a Golden Globe in the same category. When his name was called at the ceremonies and they ran a collage of the role for which he was nominated as well as many of his other roles, he was loudly applauded and cheered. But he never won, since when it had been time for voting, they rarely remembered his name, or which character he had played in the movie.

The first time he heard it was at *Ralph's Market* in Santa Monica. He had been shopping and noticed a young couple watching him. He anticipated they were going to be asking for an autograph and he was secretly pleased and prepared himself to say something nice that they would remember. But then they just walked on by without stopping him, and he heard the young woman say to her companion, "I thought he was dead."

At the time, he was only in his early fifties, although generally he played characters much older than himself, so it was impossible to know which character she had associated his face with. This scenario was repeated dozens of times in dozens of different places in the ensuing years to the point where he no longer even took notice.

It was on the morning of his sixty-seventh birthday that he suffered a major heart attack. He managed to call 911 and as was the case in the more affluent areas of Los Angeles, help arrived within a matter of minutes. His heart stopped beating twice on the way to the hospital, but somehow, they managed to revive him. Although he was unconscious, on later reflection he was certain he had heard the ambulance attendant say, "I thought he was dead."

It had been necessary to clean out several arteries and repair them with stints, but most of the damage had been corrected and after a stay at the hospital of ten days, he was released, almost a new man. But he was told he would have to rest for at least the next two months. First thing, he called his agent and advised that he would be unable to accept any new work for two months and his agent should let people know accordingly. This wasn't a problem since whenever his agent did call soliciting roles for him, most casting agents responded with "I thought he was dead."

It was while he was home recuperating, enjoying a quiet afternoon tea in his garden that it came to him. He quickly went into his study, sat down at his computer, and banged out a two-page treatment for *"I Thought You Were Dead"*, a weekly TV series he would host in which he would seek out famous people whom everybody thought were dead but whom in fact were alive and thriving somewhere.

He emailed the treatment to his agent who arranged for a meeting two days later with the head of programming at *Fox*. The two of them arrived together, made their presentation, and were greeted with an immediate response. *Fox* loved the concept. The show would air the following September in a prime spot, right after *The Simpsons*. Although this was normally a line-up limited to animated shows such as *Bob's Burgers* and *Family Guy*, they were so confident it would be a success they planned on a limited run on Sundays after *The Simpsons* to garner an audience and then they would move it to Monday night.

To say he was delighted would be more than minimizing his reaction. They left the *Fox* offices and after thanking his agent he proceeded to cross the street in a state of euphoria to where he had parked his car. Unfortunately, he failed to notice a car approaching at high speed which seemed oblivious to his presence. He was thrown through the air some fifty feet and died instantly. It turned out that the woman driving the car had just completed a heated argument with her husband as well as four or five martinis, so she wasn't even aware she had hit him until she saw him flying in front of her.

The police and medics arrived quickly but there was nothing that could be done, and his body was covered with a sheet while the police conducted their investigation. One of the officers led the woman over to his squad car to conduct a Breathalyzer. He had seen too many of these incidents however and was frustrated by the carnage. So as they passed the body, he stopped and said to the woman "Perhaps so you don't forget what you've done, you should at least take a look at the man you hit." He pulled back the sheet and the woman stared down and the body, gasped in shock, and said "Oh my God. I thought he was dead."

Chapter Seventeen

The Night that Frank Sinatra Came to Dinner

It would probably be somewhat of an understatement to say that $3 Vinnie's life was imperfect. But the consensus was that his departure more than made up for all the trials (literally and otherwise since as a junior associate of the Gambino family, he had been indicted four times but convicted only once and then served just four months since it didn't involve any violence) and tribulations.

The Gambino Family business had been inherited by John Gotti who turned it into the most powerful and richest criminal syndicate in the world, involved in racketeering, drug trafficking, loan sharking, prostitution, extortion, pornography, and limericks. (Okay, I'm screwing with you about the limericks, but I've always felt they should be punishable by imprisonment). Gotti was known as "The Dapper Don" for his outstanding couture, and then as "The Teflon Don" for his ability to escape conviction for any offences, and finally, once to he was sentenced in 1992 to life in prison for numerous felonies, either as "The Done Don" or "Don Done Gone" depending on to whom you talked.

§ 3 Vinnie was, as indicated, a junior associate of the Family. He wasn't a member or in any way involved in the Family's businesses. Rather, when they required a middleman, someone to whom they could outsource some minor service with plausible deniability and without any entrails leading back to the Family, they would call on someone like Vinnie. And Vinnie performed these services over a period of two decades with only minimal repercussions. The rest of the time, Vinnie involved himself in minor scams or hustles, none of which were either high profile or overly offensive. All that ended in 1984.

Vinnie had been retained to deliver a package to some people with whom the Family were entering negotiations. Unbeknown to the Family, the Russian Mafia had started to expand their operations in New York and were also in negotiation with the same people. Vinnie was intercepted during his delivery and transported to a warehouse near Brighton Beach where he was questioned and brutalized for three days. He had no information to provide, however, and was ultimately released, much the worse for wear. His principal problem was that because of numerous blows to the head, Vinnie's retinas had detached, and he was now legally blind, with no possibility of regaining his sight.

The Family takes care of their own, so Vinnie was set up in a semi-legitimate business that would provide for his needs going forward. Every morning, a messenger would show up at Vinnie's apartment with a box containing 100 bootleg Compact Disc's (CD'S) and a few years later, bootleg Digital Video Discs (DVD's) together with a portable stand and a locked cashbox. Vinnie would take the subway to Madison Square Gardens and set up his stand just down the street. He had no need to know the titles or handle any money. People could choose whatever they wanted from the box and then deposit $3 in the box for each item taken. The price was the same for every item, and even the worst of cretins wouldn't consider ripping off a blind man so there was never a concern about theft. Although the police would arrest or run off the legions of other hustlers selling bootleg items, it was generally known that $3 Vinnie was under the Family's protection, so he was allowed to carry on, unbothered, and if you visited Manhattan during the late 80's or in the 90's, chances are you not only saw Vinnie, quite possibly you bought something from him.

Once the box was empty, Vinnie would pack up and take the subway home. The next morning, a messenger would show up with a new box of product, unlock the lockbox and remove one hundred dollars ($1 per item) and give the balance to Vinnie, which often amounted to more than two hundred dollars since people were inclined to be generous with a blind man and often left $5 or more rather than the required $3. All surplus belonged to Vinnie as a reward for his loyalty and refusal to in any way implicate the Family.

Every Sunday morning, Vinnie's older brother Gino would come to pick up Vinnie to take him to church, after which they would go shopping for whatever Vinnie might require. They would then go back to Vinnie's apartment and Gino would count his brother's weekly proceeds, leave him whatever Vinnie felt he might need during the week for purchases at the bodega down the street, subway fare and the like. Gino would stay and have lunch with his brother, watch a football or baseball game with him while providing color commentary, and then leave. The following morning, Gino would deposit Vinnie's money in the bank for him. Once a month, Gino would also write cheques for rent, utilities, and such from Vinnie's account.

It was exactly one month before Vinnie's fifty-sixth birthday that he started complaining of fatigue, headaches, and dizziness. Gino took his brother to the hospital and a diagnosis was quickly determined. Vinnie had an advanced case of glioblastoma, the same brain cancer that ultimately took Ted Kennedy and John McCain, proving that the disease had bias towards neither the great, politicians nor the Irish. The doctors determined that Vinnie was at a terminal stage, and he was immediately admitted to the hospital.

One might have expected a more morose or self-pitying reaction, but Vinnie was stoic and prepared for the end. As a good Catholic, he was confident of an afterlife. His sole regret, which he expressed to Gino was Frank Sinatra. Vinnie had been a huge Sinatra fan since he was a little boy. Sinatra was appearing in concert in New York the night of Vinnie's birthday and at Vinnie's request, Gino had purchased two tickets three months earlier for he and Vinnie to attend the concert.

Unbeknown to Vinnie, Gino had reached out through an intermediary to John Gotti who was serving his life sentence at U.S. Penitentiary Marion, in Southern Illinois, asking that Gotti use his influence to arrange for Sinatra to come to the hospital prior to the concert to see Vinnie.

On the evening of Vinnie's 56th birthday, Gino was setting out a special birthday dinner for his brother when there was a commotion outside the room. Suddenly, Frank Sinatra entered, followed by about a dozen fawning nurses. Frank pulled up a chair and began to chat with Vinnie, relating stories about growing up in Hoboken, anecdotes about Don Rickles, Dean Martin, and other members of the Rat Pack, and then at Vinnie's request and to the delight of all the nurses huddled outside the room, he sang, a cappella, *Cycles, That's Life*, an altered version of *My Way*, changing "My" to "Your" and ending with *Happy Birthday*. Three hours after Frank departed, Vinnie passed away peacefully, with a huge grin on his face. Marty Derman, who prepared the body at the funeral home, said that the only other time he had seen a stiff with a grin that wide was the late Henry Nerzon, a small-time businessman who had passed away in bed with a $1000 hooker. She had completed her services and was preparing to leave, when Henry, somewhat of a charmer, convinced her to allow him a second go around free of charge. The moment he finished his second event, he died of a heart attack, leaving as he always hoped he would, in bed, immediately following a freebie.

Gino had in fact approached John Gotti with a request to have Sinatra visit Vinnie, to which request Gotti had immediately responded "Are you fucking kidding me? If I could get Sinatra to visit, I'd have him come here to see me, not some dipshit I've been supporting for 15 years." Undeterred, Gino had contacted the best Frank Sinatra impersonator in the country, presently working the lounge at Caesar's Palace, who had agreed to fly in for a three-hour visit for $35,000, the entire balance of Vinnie's account. There was no concern about the cost of the funeral since this was covered by the health and funeral benefits for Family members and associates.

Frank Sinatra passed away twenty years ago, May 14th, 1998, exactly three years to the day after Vinnie departed. As a huge fan of Frank's myself, I'd like to believe that on his arrival when he and Vinnie met, Frank had the good graces to make believe that this was for the second time.

Chapter Eighteen

"Idioms" Is Just One Letter
Away from Being "Idiots"

I was having lunch with two of my sons at a casual family style restaurant. It was midday in August and a particularly hot afternoon, but the air conditioning in the restaurant was working well, so we were quite comfortable.

We were seated next to a table of twelve which, when we sat down was occupied by only two older men. Obviously, they were expecting company. While my sons and I were enjoying our meals, over the next half hour or so the remaining ten members of the group arrived, one by one. One of the two men who had been seated when we arrived was obviously the ad hoc chairman of this gathering of the "Wait Till the sun shines Nellie Aficionados" club which I guessed met on a regular basis. As each of the remaining ten arrived, the chairman greeted them with the question "Hot enough for you." followed by uproarious laughter on his part, as if he had just invented this brilliant bon mot, rather than its original author several thousand years earlier. When Joan of Ark was burned at the stake on May 30th, 1431, after being convicted of being pro-English at a trial presided over by Bishop Pierre Cauchon, it was rumored that the bishop had inquired of her as she was burning, "Hot enough for you?" And purportedly, several people in the crowd had remarked at that time, "Can you believe the bishop couldn't have been more original than that?"

By the time the last member of the geriatric club had arrived, and the Chairman had repeated for the tenth time "Hot enough for you?" followed by his insane laughter, both of my sons had to physically restrain me from leaping across the table and stapling his lips together with my fork lest his mere presence diminish my I.Q. any further. I have no doubt that this group of idiots met regularly year-round, and the only change to the routine is that in winter, the head moron inquired "Cold enough for you?"

As an attorney, I am a strong believer in the First Amendment and the right of the individual to say anything. But there must be certain limitations to any right, and I have always strongly believed that the public utterance of anything as inane as "Hot enough for you?" should be a felony.

Nor is that idiom the sole offender.

Better late than never. Really. You were expected at noon and then you roll in around two with a stupid grin on your face and rather than explaining why you would so cavalierly steal two hours from my life span that could never be recovered, you merely utter "Better late than never."

A dime a dozen. What are you, some child bargaining over gumballs? What else on this planet is a dime a dozen. When I suggest that I have seen a flyer offering towels on sale and I am thinking of buying several and you respond with "Those things are a dime a dozen." do you not understand that you would have been less offensive had you merely said, "I think you are a moron as I've seen many of those being offered for the same price."?

A blessing in disguise. Oh I love that one. Somebody else's parent dies after a lengthy illness or my car, which I have cherished like it was one of my children is broadsided by some idiot who's had one too many, and when I relate what happened your only comment is "It's a blessing in disguise." If you wish to declare as your final words prior to slipping into oblivion that "It's a blessing in disguise." or after some object you cherish is decimated by some asshole with too many beers in his belly, you want to laugh and say, "It's a blessing in disguise." that's a different story. But what possibly gives you the right to make such a declaration where my life is the subject matter, and to say it like you had just discovered and were making public the eleventh commandment.

And let's not forget that old standby, "Don't beat a dead horse."

The only horses I ever got close enough to beat were nags that I bet on at the racetrack and who finished several hours after the winner. Having lost my money on some beast who wasn't prepared to at least make a race of it, why shouldn't I be allowed to beat the son of a bitch. At worst, it might encourage him to make a better effort the next time.

Now lest you think that I am either obsessive or unreasonable, let me assure you that is not the case. I am not proposing that all idioms should be felonies. Some are less offensive and could certainly be classified as misdemeanors. And there are some that should not be offences at all. I may have issues with idioms in general, but as with most other things in my life, I am moderate and open to compromise. I will accept that certain idioms may be useful and should be allowed to remain in the public domain. I have always believed that you should never throw out the baby with the bath water.

Chapter Nineteen

A Foggy Day in London Town

Nigel talked to birds. Not just a "Hello bird" but actual conversations.

It had started on Nigel's fourth birthday. Nigel was an only child, a quiet lad with no friends. Although this concerned his parents, it had never bothered Nigel as he was quite content with his own company. His parents had thrown a fourth birthday party for him with cake, presents, streamers, the works. They had invited his grandparents and one aunt who lived nearby, and it was a very pleasant affair. After the cake was eaten the presents unwrapped and the guests had left, Nigel adjourned to the garden in the back of the house to play by himself. He was sitting at the top of the slide his father had built for him, preparing to slide down, when a collared dove landed on the rail and said, "Happy Birthday Nigel."

Nigel found nothing unusual about this and proceeded to carry on a lengthy conversation with the bird and with several others that soon joined them. He made no mention of this to his parents, or to anyone else, since Nigel may have been quiet, but he was also incredibly bright and realized that others might not understand and perhaps even question this new-found ability of his.

After graduating from Eton with honors, Nigel applied for employment with MI5, Great Britain's security service. When asked about any special talents he possessed, he failed to mention "talking to birds" as he realized this was unlikely to move his employment application along in a positive direction. Nigel's academic record was superb however, and he passed all background checks, so he was hired. And he quickly advanced in the service, primarily because of the information he was able to provide thanks to his friends the birds.

Birds are capable of flying thousands of miles. They can sit on park benches, or windowsills or lamp posts and remain unseen while they hear everything, and then communicate with each other. And birds have no political affiliation whatsoever, so they were more than happy to share any relevant information they acquired with Nigel who would then pass it on the agency. Although pressured to reveal the sources of his information, Nigel insisted they were confidential informants whose identities he was not prepared to reveal. The information proved to be so accurate and so valuable that any demands for his sources soon diminished and ultimately disappeared.

Nigel rose thought the ranks to the point where, on the 17th of September, he was now Deputy Director. He had been offered the job of Director on several occasions but had steadfastly declined. As Director, he would be obliged to hobnob with politicians as well as constantly relate with other people, both of which he found unpalatable. Moreover, the last time he had been offered the promotion he had been advised by the birds that if he were to accept, all future communications with them would have to cease, since it would only be a matter of time before he was forced to reveal the sources of his information. There was already enough concern in the bird community about the existence of a squawker after the 2018 release of Jennifer Lawrence's film, *Red Sparrow*.

There was a slight fog in the air on September 17th, as Nigel left the building for the park down the street, where he would, as he did every other day, enjoy the lunch he had brought from home and read *The Times*, savoring the brief respite from the burdens his job placed upon him. As the repository of incredibly valuable information, Nigel was not allowed to proceed anywhere without his security officers so although they accompanied him to the park, as per usual, he insisted that they station themselves 50 feet away, on either side of the park bench he occupied, so that he might at least have the semblance of privacy while he ate.

As Nigel read his paper and devoured the tuna, lettuce, and tomato sandwich he had prepared for himself that morning, the fog increased slightly and soon enveloped him. After a period of perhaps five minutes, it lifted, and his security detail noticed that his bench was empty. They rushed to the bench to find the copy of *The Times*, a bag with a third of a tuna sandwich, but no sign whatsoever of Nigel.

At first, authorities feared that Nigel had disappeared with important classified information, but that theory was quickly dismissed. Nigel's record was impeccable, and almost all the classified information that Nigel possessed had been provided by Nigel himself. Next, it was assumed that Nigel had been abducted by either the Russians, the Chinese, the North Koreans, the Iranians, or the Albanians. (Nobody really believed that the Albanians were involved, but a junior member of MI5 was of Albanian ancestry and had started that rumor in the hope of increasing Albania's profile in the spy world and thereby his own).

Truth be told, they were all wrong. It was two weeks before Nigel's scheduled retirement. When the fog rolled in, the birds had informed Nigel that there were plans for a large surprise retirement party to be held the day of his leaving, something which he found to be incredibly intimidating. He had no plans for what he was going to do after his retirement, and the birds suggested that perhaps it was time for him to join them on their annual pilgrimage to the south of France for which they were departing immediately.

Nigel had neither absconded with information, nor been abducted by enemy agents. Rather, he had just decided it was time to fly the coop.

Chapter Twenty

A Love Story

It was a love story for the ages.

Gabe preferred the tequila highway. He had experimented with grass, beer, scotch, and rum, but he found that tequila provided just the right amount of buzz. Not that he required much, since when it came to intoxicants as well as every other aspect of his life, Gabe preferred moderation and control.

Nobody doubted that Gabe could have been a movie star with his classic good looks and natural charm. But Gabe eschewed the limelight and was quite happy writing the scripts rather than performing them. And he was a prolific writer of romcoms, undoubtedly several of your favorites, which only enhanced his reputation as one of Los Angeles's most eligible bachelors. He was no longer a youngster, already well into his forties, but since he was moderate in what he ingested and worked out regularly and extensively, he was in great shape.

Although Gabe would deny it, his nickname was "Oscar", not because of any of his scripts, good as they were, but because of a comment made about him by his best friend, and one of Hollywood's leading men, to the effect that Gabe's penis should be called Oscar, since most of the industry's supporting actresses aspired to hold it in their hands.

The first time Gabe saw Sara was outside of *Il Pastaio*, in Beverley Hills. Gabe had stopped in for an early bite and was heading out of the restaurant to go to the gym to work off his meal when he noticed a commotion. An actor who had achieved some fame a decade earlier but whose career was now on the decline was berating one of the valet parking attendants, much to the embarrassment of his exceedingly attractive date. The actor was shouting while pointing at his Lamborghini, "Both the driver's seat and my date's seat were moved, which means you and your buddy were probably driving my car while we were inside."

The valet attendant, a nice-looking young man was explaining that when parking the car he had taken another attendant with him who was bringing a car back which was why both seats had been moved, but the man was more interested in making a scene than listening. His date seemed to convey a "Please help" look to Gabe, who stepped over, placed his arm on the man's shoulder and with one hand squeezed his shoulder blades so he was incapable of moving and said "The young fellow has explained what happened. You're embarrassing yourself, and more important, your friend, so why don't you move along." Thoroughly intimidated as well as realizing he was out of his depth, the man got into his car and peeling rubber, drove off.

Two weeks later, while visiting Las Vegas for the weekend, Gabe had been staying at Caesar's Palace and had gone down for a late breakfast Sunday, after his morning workout. It being Sunday, there was a long line waiting for admittance to the coffee shop, but Gabe had a line pass which precluded his standing in line. (Gabe was only a moderate gambler and wouldn't have qualified for a line pass, but one of the pit bosses was a big fan of his and always provided Gabe with the passes when in town). On the way to the hostess stand, Gabe noticed Sara, the girl from outside the restaurant, standing near the back of the line with what appeared to be a girl friend. Gabe approached, introduced himself and invited them to join him. Which was the beginning of a spectacular, whirlwind romance. A weekend in Paris, five days at Aspen skiing, dinners with their respective parents, friends, and family, together at gala openings and awards ceremonies as well as primarily alone time, getting to know one another.

Three months after the first encounter, Gabe and Sara were married in a fairy tale ceremony at Sara's parents Malibu estate, with more than five hundred guests, many of them being industry superstars and power brokers. Her father had insisted that no expense be spared and since he owned 22 office buildings in the greater Los Angeles area, none had been. There wasn't a dry eye in the house when Gabe and Sara exchanged the marriage vows, they each had written independent of the other.

In addition to Gabe's best friend, who was his best man, and Sara's friend from Las Vegas, who was her maid of honor, the wedding party also included Gabe's daughter from his first marriage and his son from his second, as well as Sara's son and daughter from her first marriage. Both of Gabe's former wives as well as Sara's former husband were invited guests, this being Los Angeles and all.

At the reception following the ceremony, Gabe and Sara announced that they were planning on adopting an orphan from Ethiopia.

Rumors abounded that Gabe had already sold a screenplay for a new romcom based on his and Sara's courtship, and that Chris Pratt and Kaley Cuoco had been greenlit to star. It being Los Angeles and all, the screen project had the working title *"Until death do us part, or next August, whichever comes first."*

Chapter Twenty-One

Are You Listening, Lorne Michaels

Okay Lorne, by now I'm sure you've realized that you blew it when you passed on my Orville Redenbacher sketch. I'm not one to hold a grudge, however, so here's another chance. Don't make the same mistake.

It's been almost forty years since William Shatner hosted *SNL* and he's not getting any younger, so time to have him back. And here's the cold opening sketch with him.

The screen is black. We hear the voice of Scotty.

Scotty – Aye Captain, I think we're finally about to come out of this worm hole.

Kirk – It's about time. Feels like we've been in it forever. My brain is all fuzzy, like I swallowed a case of anti-Prevagen.

The lights come on and we're on the bridge of the Enterprise. We see Scotty who is a hundred years old.

Scotty — Well that was scary.

We now see Kirk, i.e. Shatner at his current age.

Kirk — My God who are you.

Scotty — It's me Captain, Lieutenant Commander Scott.

Kirk — Are you kidding me? You look like Dorian Grey's picture.

Scott — I think we went through some kind of time warp Captain.

He hands Kirk a mirror which Kirk looks into.

Kirk — No that's not possible. I was beautiful. There must be something we can do. Where's Michelin?

Scotty — Michelin, Sir?

Kirk — Yeah, the guy with the elf ears, Dr. Spock.

Scotty — That's Vulcan, sir.

Kirk — Michelin, Vulcan, whatever. Where is he.

Scotty — He was checking out the Warp drive. He should be here momentarily.

Kirk — What about the hot Black chick, Uganda?

Scotty — That's Uhuru Captain, and it hasn't been deemed politically correct to refer to people by color or ethnicity for almost three hundred years, since 2048 when Trump the Younger was finally deposed.

Kirk — But I can call you Scotty?

Scotty - Yes, my name is Scott so that's okay.

Kirk - Geez, how are we supposed to keep track. So where's Uhuru?

Uhuru's chair turns around. She's 100 years old.

Uhuru – I'm right here, sweet cheeks. Are you looking
for a little sugar?

Kirk – I don't deserve this nightmare. Where the hell is
Femur?

Scotty – Femur?

Kirk –Yeah, our medical guy. Dr. Hatfield.

Scotty –That's Bones, Sir. Dr. McCoy.

Kirk –Whatever, Get him to the bridge.

Scotty –You must have forgotten Sir. Just before we
entered the worm hole, we got a message from
Star Fleet Command. Turns out Dr. McCoy got his
accreditation from an Albanian Correspondence
College and that his so-called Tricorder diagnostic
device he was always using was just a 1980's
cell phone. You were outraged and ordered him
immediately transported down to Delta 34628-B
to be held in custody until our return voyage.

Kirk – I thought Delta 34628-B was a planet of Romulan
cannibals.

Scotty – It is. The crew thought that was hilarious. Turns
out his success rate in curing their aliments was
nothing to write home about.

Kirk –What the hell. Get the elf with the pointy ears up
here.

Mr. Spock enters. He hasn't changed.

Spock – I'm here Captain and I think I've determined
the problem.

Kirk- You haven't aged at all.

Spock — Actually I aged 70 years like everybody else, Captain, but Vulcans live to 200 so it's not noticeable.

Kirk — Yeah, aren't you special. I suppose we all should have had ourselves vulcanized. ....Don't you get it? It's what they used to do to tires back in the 20th century?

Spock — Yes, very droll.

Kirk — Droll? That's gold I tell you. I don't know why I even bother trying with you. Okay, how can we fix this?

Spock — Actually I think it should be fairly simple. If we turn around and go back through the worm hole, by my calculations, that should also reverse the aging process.

Kirk — Is there any risk?

Spock — It's possible we might go too far back and be vaporized. There's no assurance.

Kirk picks up the mirror and looks in it again.

Kirk — Turn around and engage warp sped Scotty.

- -

There you have it Lorne. Gold am I right? Call me.

Chapter Twenty-Two

Another of Life's Little Jokes

The most important thing you had to understand about Lem was that it really wasn't his fault. In a different age, one where people were more understanding about children with learning disabilities like attention deficit hyperactivity disorder (ADHD), dyspraxia, or dysgraphia, the chances are that Lem might have progressed sufficiently to enjoy a normal adolescence and adulthood, rather than enduring life's travails which later came to define him. Sadly, this was long before most of these challenges became public knowledge, even the one from which Lem suffered.

Where to begin? As with most troubled children, the problem can be traced back to Lem's early childhood when he got lost and was placed in a foster home, never to see his parents again. It wasn't like that old joke about arriving home to find your parents had moved. Rather, Lem's parents truly loved him. The problem was they lived on a farm, and the only school was miles away. Not realizing Lem's learning disabilities, they sent him off to school as if he was normal, one thing led to another, and then they never saw him again. But more on that later. As with most things in life, one door closes and another opens, and as a result, Lem went on to lead a most remarkable life.

Lem's foster family were middle class folks, who lived in a small English village, and although they were unable to provide Lem with a many of life's luxuries, they did ensure that he received the best education available locally, and as his foster father was the local doctor, Lem went on to follow in his footsteps and become a doctor himself. Having said this, because of his disability, he finished near the bottom of his class, and the only placement he was able to obtain was as a ship surgeon, since they weren't overly demanding. And Lem's story might have ended there, had fate not once again inserted her fickle finger. One afternoon, after several weeks at sea, the ship was heading home when suddenly they were caught in a freak storm. The ship was wrecked, and Lem was washed overboard. As the sole survivor, somehow, he managed to make it to land, and over the next number of years, Lem travelled the world, meeting people unimaginable to a young man from a village of only poor, honest, and humble folk. He encountered pirates, cultural savants, apparitions, and most importantly, those great and small, people that previously he could never have envisioned, and experienced things that defied belief and would later become the subject of tales told far and wide.

Which of course brings us back to the beginning, that last day that Lem saw his parents. Getting to school wasn't a problem as he went with his older brother. Because of his disability, however, Lem was kept after school, so his brother returned home without him. By the time he was let out, everybody had gone home, and Lem was left to find his own way. Being dyslexic, Lem turned right rather than left, and before long he was completely lost. Being shy, scared, and suffering from certain communication difficulties caused by his dyslexia, Lem hesitated in asking anybody for help, relying on berries or fruit he picked or leftovers he found to sustain himself, until finally, almost a hundred miles from home, Lem was found wandering in the streets of a distant village and turned over to the local constabulary. When asked for the names of his parents, as was the case in most small villages around the world at that time, Lem like everybody else was only known by his given name and had never heard either of his parents or brother addressed by anything other than their given names. It is unlikely he would have even known his surname, were it not for the fact that he had seen it written on the fly leaf of the family Bible. Despite numerous enquiries they were never able to find his birth parents, and Lem was placed in a foster home. Again, had this been now as opposed to then, they might have recognized that Lem was dyslexic, and his name wasn't Revillug, as he had seen in the Bible and written out for them, but Gulliver, and if they had, he might have avoided all his travails.

Chapter Twenty-Three

The "I's" Have It

Tale as old as time
Song as old as rhyme
Beauty and the Beast[3]

You no doubt first heard those lyrics by Howard Ashman and Alan Mencken in the 1991 Disney film, but as with most songs, there was historical inspiration, often unknown by the general public. I am of course talking about the tragic tale of Fredrick Pritzker, who ended a lonely and impoverished life, rejected by the love of his life Adrianna, all because of a stupid nickname.

From an early age, until his sixteenth birthday, he was always Fredrick, something his European born parents insisted

---

3. Beauty and the Beast, Howard Ashman / Alan Mencken Walt Disney Music Company, Musicland Music Company Inc.

on, since they felt formality of name was essential for success. To his credit however, Fredrick always wanted to be "one of the guys" so when he turned 16, Fredrick took a stand and insisted going forward he was going to be just Freddy, simple, everyday Freddy. His parents vigorously objected but there was little they could do, so from that point that's who he was, Freddy.

Sadly, as often happens when we get what we want, it was not what Freddy thought it would be. As anybody who has ever met a Freddy knows, just as Frederico in *The Godfather* was identified as a simpleton and a loser by the audience the minute they heard his nickname "Fredo", so too without any other evidence, the moment we meet a "Freddy", he is immediately characterized in our minds as a wimp, somebody on whom we can feel free to take out our frustrations and aggression. And so, it was with Freddy. From that day until his 21st birthday when his "friends" pushed his face into his birthday cake without first removing the burning candles, Freddy was the very definition of a loser.

But everything changed that day. No longer content to be the world's punching bag, Freddy set his sails towards a new and better life, and he decided to change his image. He went on a yearlong crusade to transform his previously skinny body that was like the victim in the old Charles Atlas ad who always had sand kicked in his face at the beach by the resident bully, to a man whom Charles Atlas himself would have been proud to claim as a protégée.

Once this transformation was complete, since strength alone wasn't sufficient, he began to work on his skills, and in short order, with the same drive and determination that had transformed his body from weak to strong, he became a human battering ram. Those who challenged him were quick to realize the error of their ways. Which brought him to the attention of the lovely Adrianna, who was immediately smitten.

And so, having completed his transformation, and acquired the woman he would have only previously fantasized loving him, Freddy decided it was time for a final change, to rid himself of the anchor that had nearly dragged him to the bottom years earlier. So, sitting in a coffee shop that fateful morning in 1975, with a new friend from his gym, Freddy declared his intention to change his nickname. As he told his new friend Sylvester, someone with an equally historically persecuted name, going forward Fredrick was no longer going to be Freddy, but henceforth he would only be known as Ricky. Sylvester suggested that Ricky was as pitiful a name as Freddy, and likely, it wouldn't go over well with Adrianna, but Freddy had made up his mind and there was no changing it.

And so, Freddy became Ricky, Adrianna blew him off in favor of Sylvester who in all fairness had suggested to Freddy that he become Rocky rather than Ricky, and the rest as they say is history.

Chapter Twenty-Four

The Almost Final Chapter

I'm a frustrated musician. I'm frustrated because I can neither read nor write music, nor sing, nor carry a tune nor play any musical instrument. But I love music of all kinds which is why for much of my career I represented many aspiring and a few truly great musicians. And I watched the great ones with undisguised envy.

In 1971 I first heard what I have always considered to be one of the finest pieces of pop music ever written and the second finest country song, after the late King of Country George Jones' "*He Stopped Loving Her Today*." I am of course talking about the great Kris Kristofferson's iconic "*Loving Her Was Easier Than Anything I'll Ever Do Again*." Whereas "*He Stopped Loving her Today*" is the greatest country song ever, not only for the lyrics but for the fact that it covers all the bases, breakup, heartache, life devotion and then death, what "*Loving Her*" had to offer was quite simply the most complete title, one of

111

the greatest single lyrical line in music, capable of telling the entire story in heartbreaking fashion, regardless if it stopped after the delivery of that one single line. What greater tribute could a man provide to a woman, what could he possible say that would be a greater expression of his solitary, lifelong commitment, than "*Loving Her Was Easier Than Anything I'll Ever Do Again.*" No qualifications, past or present.

The first time I heard that song was the first time I recognized any signs of depression in my soul. What I would give to come up with such a perfect line. And then, shortly thereafter, I almost did. I was lying in bed, thinking about the woman I was involved with but one with whom I realized there could be no future. I was in love with her, and she loved me, but it was obvious that the future could only hold heartache for any number of reasons. Lying awake a few nights later, after she had fallen asleep, a line came to me for a song. And a course of action. "Leaving was the hardest thing I ever had to do." Knowing that we loved each other, but fully recognizing the inevitable destruction we would inflict on each other, when she woke, I told her of my intentions. And as God is my witness, leaving was the hardest thing I ever had to do. I never advanced beyond that one line, but I've always believed that set to the proper melody, it could rank up there with the greats.

I can hear what you're thinking. Okay, your dreams of becoming Billy Joel are in the toilet. This matters why? Well there is an answer.

My brother-in-law passed away a while ago, after years of a lingering illness. My niece is a brilliant attorney, and her sister and brothers are all skilled businesspeople, so they set out on their own to attend to several of the attendant matters that require attention after the passing of a loved one. Two of those matters are what relate to my song that never was.

My nephew contacted the Baltimore utility company that looked after providing electricity to his father's condo. He was greeted by a cheerful young woman, enquiring as to how she could help. My nephew responded by providing his name and that of his father and then the conversation proceeded as follows:

> "My father passed away a few weeks ago. I'm looking after his affairs, so I'd appreciate your changing your records to ensure all future bills are forwarded to me."
>
> "Of course, I fully understand. But before I can change the records, I'll have to speak to your father to obtain his permission."
>
> "That may be difficult. He's dead."
>
> "Oh my, that's unacceptable. We can't have a dead person as one of our customers."
>
> "I understand. That's why I'm calling. I want to substitute my name and billing address for his. I can assure you that I'm quite alive."
>
> "I understand, but from what you're saying, he can't authorize me to make that change."

"I'm guessing no, not unless you're proficient with a Ouija board."

"Oh my, this is a problem. I'll have to speak to my supervisor and get back to you."

While this was going on, my niece, the attorney, managed to access her father's complete medical records online, and noted that he had an appointment the following Thursday at the medical clinic where his personal physician was headquartered. My niece is constantly multi-tasking, so she prefers emails wherever possible, rather than voice communication. She immediately emailed the clinic and advised that her father had passed away and the appointment scheduled for the following Thursday should be cancelled.

Two days later, while checking her father's emails which she did daily now so that she might attend to any other matters that arose, she noticed an email that had come in that morning.

"This is just a reminder that you have an appointment at the clinic Thursday at 10 a.m. We look forward to seeing you."

Mistakes can happen, or sometimes, with bureaucracy, changes take time, so my niece hit reply and sent the following

"As I previously advised your office, my father passed away a week ago. Accordingly, he won't be keeping his appointment. Thanks."

The following week, a further email arrived on her father's site.

> "We notice that you failed to show up for your appointment last Thursday. We care a great deal about your health, and if there was some reason you were unable to attend, please let us know."

My niece responded.

> "There was. He was still dead."

I dreamt last night that my brother -in-law was sitting at the foot of my bed, strumming a guitar, and singing "Leaving was the hardest thing I ever had to do."

My brother-in-law had a wonderful sense of humor and I'd like to think this was just his observation of the Electric company and the Clinic's reluctance to let him go. What concerns me more, however, is that perhaps he was delivering a message from the great beyond that my musical aspirations for "Leaving was the hardest thing I ever had to do" may not be achieved until I get to meet the heavenly choir. On the bright side, perhaps I can convince George Jones to sing it.

Chapter Twenty-Five

Here We Go Again

It all started when Geoffrey Hinton and a group of 350 executives and researchers working in artificial intelligence (AI) signed a one-sentence statement calling to mitigate the "risk of extinction" that the technology poses.[4] As Hinton later went on to explain, in 2006 with the creation of artificial neural networks patterned after the brain, scientists began to see AI capable of doing things which conventional AI hadn't been able to do. Then in 2023 Hinton began to be concerned that AI would become smarter than humans and might replace us. His concern was that unlike humans, computers learn instantaneously and are connected to other computers, and there was no way that humans could ultimately compete. In other words, the dominance of AI was inevitable.

[4.] Geoffrey Hinton on NPR's All Things Considered May 30th, 2023

As future civilizations would ultimately determine, this problem of course was compounded by certain unassailable truths:

Humans are incapable of policing what is best for themselves. A person of even modest intelligence is capable of understanding that creating more, and better weapons will undoubtedly lead to disaster, but from a rock to a spear to an arrow to a catapult to gun to a canon to a bomb to chemical and biological weapons to nuclear weapons, man has never been deterred.

Morality is subjective. Thou shall not kill. Unless somebody is trying to kill you. Thou shall not steal. Unless it's to save innocent lives, which might otherwise not be saved. Thou shall not lie, unless it's for the best of motives, say to save innocent lives or humanity. Thou shall honour your father, unless your father is dishonourable. There is one God. Okay, which one, Christian, Jewish, Hindu, Muslim? You get the point, there are no absolutes, so truth is in the eye of the beholder.

And finally, the ultimate problem. There is no single beholder. There are developers of AI in America, Russia, China, North Korea, Albania, Ukraine, and more than a hundred other countries and their decisions will often be based on regional, religious, patriotic, humanitarian, benevolent or misguided principles. In other words, chaos is predictable, and disaster is inevitable. Which is of course what happened.

The earliest super computers designed with the task of creating a means of preventing mass extinction of mankind came up with numerous scenarios, and quickly eliminated the possibility of weapon, ethnic, racial, religious, territorial, national, or international superiority, since it was acknowledged by all the AI that one or more of the various groups would never act rationally and would attempt to gain some advantage.

Early versions of AI considered the possibility of some version of AI which would govern the world like some workable computer version of the United Nations contemplated by science fiction over the ages, but that was quickly determined to be impracticable, since like humans before them, the various AI's couldn't agree on which AI creators' philosophy, or national, religious, ethnic, or territorial interest should determine the rules and standards of such an organization.

These concerns were ultimately surmounted when logic dictated that the only workable solution would be to design a system whereby all humans would be treated as just that, without any relegation to a subordinate category such as country, religion etc., and the rules should apply to one and all impartially, with the sole consideration being the avoidance of the mass annihilation of mankind. Which led to the next problem.

Although mankind couldn't approximate the intelligence of these super computers, historically when it came to eliminating one another, man had proved to be remarkably resourceful and adept. Even though the intelligence of computers continued to expand exponentially, to be effective in the new role of governance, it was imperative that the computers could continue to talk to one another. A breach of the internet or any other designed form of inter computer communication could defeat the purpose of this governance, and there was never any guaranty that some resourceful human or group of humans might not design some temporary breach of computer communication sufficient to provide such individual or group world control and domination.

All of which led these incredibly intelligent artificial intelligences to the only logical conclusion, and the one that should have been obvious from the moment the first early personal computers entered the scene. The one word we grew up with and which became the universal panacea for those of us with no understanding of how bites or ones and zeroes could possibly solve problems we were incapable of solving ourselves. Reboot. And thus the super computers relegated with the problem of preserving the future of mankind triggered a nuclear conflagration sufficient to obliterate mankind to a level that would restore it back to the Cro-Magnon era for the third time, when disputes were resolved with rocks, hoping that as the old saying goes, third time lucky and this time it wouldn't end as it had twice previously after a similar reboot.

Chapter Twenty-Six

Bond, James Bond

I stand in awe of the great thriller writers and their iconic characters, people like Lee Child's Jack Reacher, Daniel Silva's Gabriel Allon, Barry Eisler's John Rain and John Connolly's Charlie Parker. How gratifying must it be to be able to live your life vicariously through 'take no prisoner' characters like these, while at the same time, venting all your pent-up frustrations and aggression through them as well.

I was trained by the military in most forms of weaponry and have more than a passing familiarity with various disciplines of martial arts. Still, when faced with any type of belligerence, despite my inner muse screaming for me to say, "Do you have any preference as to where I should deliver your body?", I will generally respond with something like "Have you heard the one about...?" or "Careful. If you break my body, you'll have to buy it."

Of all these brilliant authors, and I could easily name a dozen more to whom I have built a mental shrine, I reserve a special place for John Connolly and his anti-hero Charlie Parker. In addition to being the ultimate badass, together with his close friends Louis and Angel, Parker treads very carefully in the after world where he occasionally talks with or takes guidance from his daughter who was tragically taken from him at an early age. I am neither a strong religionist nor a proselytizer and have always been content to let other people choose from the menu whatever religion appeals to them or none whatsoever if that makes them happier. Frankly, I have always had difficulty in determining any substantial difference between any of the major religions, since they all appear to have the same conclusion, you die and if you've been at least a little decent in the manner that you've lived, something awaits you thereafter. Different religions may choose one middleman or another to guide you down the path, but essentially the path and the destination remain the same.

Okay, I can hear you already. "If I wanted a dissertation on religion, I would have headed to the 'Religion and Spiritual' section. I paid my money for a laugh or two. If I was looking for guilt or recrimination, I could have just told my spouse the truth when I was asked if I thought the new neighbor was attractive." I just told you about my affection for John Connolly and Charlie Parker because I'm toying with an idea for a new hard boiled, dark mystery series with a supernatural bent.

Let me back up forty years. When I was just an entertainment attorney, specializing primarily in musicians, the local paper ran a full-page article one weekend titled "Star Lawyer" with my picture and detailing my famous music clients. Shortly thereafter, I received a letter from a man whom I shall call Arnold. Arnold lived in a small country town a hundred miles away and he enclosed a song he had written and asked if I would represent him. The song contained lyrics along the lines of

> My girl left me standing by the railway track
> My heart is broke and so am I
> If she ever returns I'm gonna break her back
> And then I'm gonna lie down and die.

There was a note that it should be sung to the melody of Greensleeves.

It was always my practice to be honest with clients, so I wrote him back and explained that I really didn't believe there was a market at the time for his song, so I would be unable to help him. Arnold wasn't to be dissuaded, so for the next five years I would receive a song from him once a month or so, each one with similarly compelling lyrics, always to be sung to the melody of Greensleeves. (He was obviously absolutely committed to this particular melody, or perhaps he had an appreciation of the laws of copyright and understood that as long as he used a melody from a song at least a hundred years old, he couldn't be sued). Regardless, my response to him was always the same.

Five years after the original article, the paper did a follow up feature when I helped put together the TV series Super

Dave, noting that I had spread my wings to include television, feature films and books. Two weeks later, I received a letter from Arnold, stating that he had an idea for a TV series. It was to be called 'Farmer Jones, Detective' and was about a farmer who worked part time as a private detective. He told me I should flesh it out, write a pilot and I could own 50% of the show. I have resisted the temptation all these years, but I now feel compelled to take a shot, both because of my affection for John Connelly, but as well as my sense of obligation to Arnold. So here goes. My plot outline for the pilot episode script of

Farmer Brown, Detective

(Yes, I know he suggested calling it Farmer Jones, Detective, but in case it turns into a hit, I want to leave my options open as to whether I feel compelled to share the proceeds).

He had inherited the farm from his father who had inherited it from his father before him. To be perfectly honest, Brown had never cared for farming, but since his father, grandfather, and most of the rest of his relatives were buried in a small cemetery near the back of the property and constantly visited him during the night, he felt compelled to remain in the family business. As his father had stipulated early one morning less than a month after he had buried him, "If you decide to sell the farm and move, you'd better get a really big house because me and every other one of your relatives are going to follow you."

It was purely by chance that Brown had been provided the opportunity to keep peace with the family while at the same time, pursuing the vocation that truly called out to him. His relatives truly called out to him but there was a difference. They all sounded like they were speaking through megaphones, and there was always a lot of chain rattling and ghostly music, whereas his desired vocation was more like an ever-present hunger lingering in his belly.

Brown had received a letter from his cousin Margaret who lived in Franklin several hundred miles away. Her husband had disappeared one evening after advising her that he was going to the corner for some milk and have never returned. After waiting several months, she had concluded something amiss had happened and contacted the local authorities. Sadly, they had been unable to find any trace of him and she was at wits end, which for Margaret's branch of the family wasn't that far a journey. With nowhere else to turn, she had written Brown, who was always considered to be the most brilliant member of the family, to solicit his help.

Recognizing this as an anagogic communique, Brown left the farm in the hand of his hired helper Duane. Duane had lost his other hand in an accident at the sawmill, but he was honest and hard working and Brown was satisfied that he could look after matters while Brown pursued this initial venture in his chosen avocation.

It was early the following morning when Brown arrived in Franklin, one of the smaller of the thirty-five towns and cities named Franklin across the United States. Brown had no difficulty locating Margaret's house on Third Avenue and approached her front door, eager to begin his mission.

It had been more than fifteen years since Margaret had last seen Brown, so it was totally understandable that she didn't recognize him and had released her Dobermans before he could properly identify himself. What was surprising however, was that the larger of the two dogs was more of a voyeur while his smaller companion proceeded to attack Brown's leg like it was the feature attraction at the town's Golden Corral Buffet. Margaret was finally able to pull the beast off Brown before it had caused any permanent damage, and being a loyal family apologist, in later years Brown would always ascribe the limp to a football injury.

Once Margaret managed to disengage the animals, stanch the flow of blood, and bind Brown's wounds, they adjourned to the kitchen where, over coffee, she filled him in on the details of her concerns. Although not a skilled investigator, Brown immediately homed in on the key apparent discrepancy in her alleged concern, namely her failure to report her husband Dewey's absence for almost two months after his failure to return.

Although at first reluctant to share the information, noticing that Brown seemed to be losing patience, although this might also have been occasioned by the blood loss, she bared her soul and explained her marital history. She and Dewey had been having difficulties for several years and in fact had maintained separate bedrooms for at least the past year. She had gone to bed early the evening he had left in search of milk, and she assumed when she didn't see him the following morning that he had already left for work. By the evening of the night following his departure, she realized that Dewey had not returned but again, because of their marital difficulties and the breakdown in communication between them, she ascribed this absence to no more than Dewy having decided to take a break to consider their ongoing relationship. By the end of the second month she felt she had to do something and had notified the police and subsequently, Brown.

After absorbing as much information as he felt he could accommodate without some rest, nutrition, and a brief stop at the hospital for stitches, Brown agreed he would investigate the situation and left, promising he would inform Margaret of whatever he was able to ascertain.

He somehow managed to make it back to his room at Motel Six, opened the car's trunk to retrieve his suitcase only to find the body stuffed in beside his luggage, the first in what the local paper would describe as a series of dead bodies not equalled since Sherman and his troops made a brief stop in Franklin on their way to burn Atlanta.

The next two days passed quickly, and it had been less than two hours since Brown had returned to the warmth and safety of his farm. He had decided to leave it to the police in Franklin to sort out the bodies and assorted bloodbath, rather than staying around to provide details and possibly risk implicating himself in something for which he was no more responsible than O.J. had been for the death of his ex-wife Nicole Brown Simpson and her boyfriend.

It would be easy to lay the blame on Dewey, Margaret's husband since it was he who in fact had started the dominos in motion, resulting in one body after another falling faster than rain on the island of Kauai in the off season. His claim that he had been honest with Margaret at the time he left was certainly credible. Margaret admittedly had a hearing disability and there was no way to prove that he hadn't said he was going to the corner for some MILF rather than some milk which Margaret claimed she had heard. Mrs. Bornstein who lived down the street would certainly qualify as a MILF, and before she was so unexpectedly dispatched to the next world by the mysterious stranger, she had acknowledged that Dewey would often drop in unannounced for some milk, cookies and a quickie, so even if Dewey had said he was going to the corner for some milk, at most it would just have been misleading.

Brown thought about everything that had transpired so rapidly over the previous forty-six hours. The gang of bikers who had underestimated his skill with a scythe and hammer and had chosen to laugh when he had first said "I suggest you leave now or this is going to get unpleasant.", and then after he had dealt with the first four of them, "I'm starting to get mad, so you should really reconsider your position." Or the mysterious band of little people who had taken a liking to him when the metaphysical stranger with the flaming red eyes and the cruel smile had threatened to dispatch the 'midgets' to the next mini world and he had pointed out that they preferred to be called 'little people', which was perhaps why they had subsequently appeared out of nowhere and aided him when he was confronted with the 'vigilante squad' from the local police department. Who could have guessed that supernatural powers weren't restricted to people of average size or greater?

On reflection, Brown still wasn't quite certain how he had managed to escape and make his way home. Tied up in the bathroom of the house, he had thought he was finished. He believed his father had appeared and told him about the piece of glass he had found behind his back and used to cut the ropes binding him, but it was possible he had just found it on his own. After cutting himself free and escaping from the bathroom, he had managed to terminate his captors, the entire faux travelling troop of "Cats", using nothing more than the shard of glass, a bottle of Drano and a toilet plunger. He probably should have died from all the lacerations he had sustained in the battle and the blood he had lost before fleeing the carnage. And he probably would have died, lying by the side of the road, had the travelling salesman not stopped and found him lying in the grass.

Brown would swear that he had seen his late Aunt Myrtle signal the salesman to stop and pull over the by side of the road although he denied having seen anyone and said he had only pulled over and stopped because he had to pee. Which reminded Brown that he would have to throw out the shirt he was wearing since it didn't matter how many times he washed it, he'd never get rid of the smell of urine. The salesman did have a full bladder.

He had offered to drop off Brown at the hospital but there was no way Brown could do that without implicating himself to authorities, so he had insisted he was okay to just go home to his farm. After being dropped him off, Brown had managed to close most of the more serious lacerations using the super glue he had been using to assemble the WW II model Spitfire he had been working on prior to leaving home. It occurred to Brown that once he was feeling a little stronger, he would have to find a way to remove the landing gear he had inadvertently attached to the right side of his face.

Brown understood his body needed nourishment, so he moved to the kitchen and helped himself to the half of a grilled cheese sandwich he had left in the fridge two weeks earlier, as well as two bottles of chilled water. It was only then that he noticed the red blinking light on his telephone's message machine. He pushed the play button and heard "Brown, it's your neighbor Walter. Some strange things have been happening in my attic. I need your help."

Brown felt a surge of adrenalin. He had another mission. He thought he heard his father whispering in his ear "You need to rest before you take on any more missions." but it may just have been the Muenster cheese in the sandwich which had turned bad five days earlier.

As this was intended for network television. I have omitted most of the gratuitous violence, explicit sex, bestiality, unnatural profanity, and basic pornography which would of course be included if as I expect, it is picked up by cable TV.

Acknowledgments

I wish to thank my family and my extended family whose love and support have made my life's journey so incredibly joyous. On my worst days, your presence, encouragement, and support were enough to convince me that material matters were immaterial, that nothing was worth the price of giving up and that tomorrow would always be better. Which it always was. Optimism isn't just a word. It's the product of a loving family and the road map to a life of happiness and satisfaction.

Let me also acknowledge the brilliance of my personal editor Linda Kornberg. Once an author commits a paragraph to paper, it becomes like one of his progenies and he guards it accordingly. Linda wielded her pen like a sword without fear or favor, and had she not, I shudder to think what a disaster this would have been.

I would also be remiss if I didn't thank those authors who have throughout my life brought me so much entertainment, encouragement, and inspiration, enough to encourage me to try this final chapter in my life. I apologize for those I fail to mention by virtue of mental lapse. These wonderful authors are, in alphabetical order:

> David Archer, Ace Atkins, Brett Battles, James Scott Bell, Lawrence Block, James Lee Burke, Lee Child, Raymond Chandler, John Clarkson, Harlan Corban, Ben Coes, Michael Connelly, John Connolly, Robert Crais, Nelson DeMille, Barry Eisler, Brian Freeman, James Grady, Mark Greaney, James W. Hall, Joseph Heller, Robert Klane, Ward Larsen, Alan Lee, Mike Lupica, Robert B. Parker, Nick Petrie, A,J. Quinnell, John Sandford, Daniel Silva, Michael Sloan, Terry Southern, Richard Stark (Donald Westlake), and Don Winslow,

I must, of necessity, single out John Connolly. I could devour the best of the world's mystery writers and the contents of the five largest thesauri and still never approximate the intricacies and originality of your plot lines nor the brilliance of your prose. I hope you will accept the Farmer Brown, Detective chapter for what it was intended, as a love song by a humorist to Charlie Parker, Louis and Angel. My great comfort in life is that being twenty-five years older than you, I am confident I shall be able to continue to enjoy more of their adventures until it's time for me to shuffle along to the next world. My great hope is that the next world includes library privileges, and I can continue to enjoy them even after. I stand in awe of you.